FORESIGHT

Book One of The Helios Oracles

PATTI LARSEN

ONE

I walk the streets of Los Angeles with a purpose, though were that reason known, I doubt anyone in my life would understand.

His face is in my mind and has been for as long as I can remember, about as long as hers. The woman I thought was the Dark One. My enemy, my family's enemy, I was told.

I think I've always had a feeling, a private and frightening foreknowledge, that the things I've been told about the future I see aren't exactly the truth.

I pass down Rodeo Drive, ignoring the expensive store fronts, the endless line of flashy sports cars, the chattering women on their smartphones. The sound of stilettos making clicking sounds on the sidewalk as they pass. I have no care for the people of this city, except their existence proves to me I'm real. I'm here. I'm not a figment of my own imagination, nor are the visions I carry inside me some false promise—and curse—of what is to come.

It's so easy to fall into melancholy as I brush past a trio of giggling girls with their perfectly styled hair, tiny dogs perched in dangling bags. Living accessories of the rich and want-to-be-noticed. How simple their lives are, without the complexities of carrying the future of the world in their heads.

I shake out my dark hair as I turn a corner and head for downtown. These stolen moments outside the sanctuary where I live, just walking, are the only real break I have from what I can do. My heart flutters, wondering if he'll show, if I'll see him today or if I'll have to return home before he appears. We've tried to schedule moments, brief but beautiful. It seems no matter our intentions neither of us are able to keep a date.

And so, I risk these trips to the surface just in case he might be here to greet me in the streets of Los Angeles. Though not exactly forbidden to me, my grandmother's hawk eye caution around me makes the sanctuary feel less a safe haven and more a prison the older and stronger I become in my power.

There was a time I felt in awe of the wonders of the world above, and hoped maybe this amazing place would somehow dim the futures I see. But the visions still come, sometimes when I least expect, taking over and drawing me into the fire that feeds them. I don't begrudge my Oracle power, nor do I ignore the importance of what I do, who I am. But there are times I wish this gift had chosen another. A simple life would be so sweet to live.

A life with my darling Piers. I sigh softly to myself as my sandals scuff the sidewalk, his sweet face on my mind.

Then again, were I like those simpering girls, I may never have met him. I bite the inside of my cheek to keep from smiling to myself as I think of the tall, blond sorcerer. Of his angular face and lean body, gray eyes as familiar as my own, the depth of his voice delicious with an English accent. He doesn't know, at least not yet, to what extent I've seen the two of us together. He might be aware of my Oracle power, but I've never confessed to Piers I've been seeing him in my head my entire life.

Piers. I cling to the name, the identity paired with his face. For many years I had no idea who he was, why he was important enough for the visions to show him to me. I had guesses, considering the content of the foresight. My cheeks pink and I cough into my hand, looking left and right with embarrassment as I pass pedestrians completely oblivious to the naughty thoughts running through my head and warming my skin. I've waited a long time to be older, to be the woman I have seen in my visions, the woman he embraces and kisses and whispers of love.

Long enough.

The first time I saw him, in a dark alley not far from where I now walk, I was certain I would blurt out my feelings for him—those ghostly, amorphous emotions clinging to the visions I'd carried with me since puberty struck. Instead, I stared, like a fool. Only the presence of Kayden, the young sorcerer with whom I'd arrived in that place, saved me from making an utter fool of myself.

I still wonder what would have happened if I'd confessed everything to Piers that night, two years ago. To him and his werewolf friend, Charlotte. Instead, I ran from him, from both of them. But my connection to Piers and my worry for his friend woke the visions and sent me a powerful foresight about Charlotte I couldn't resist. I risked everything going to them, sharing what I'd seen about the werewoman and her fate. But even as I did what I could to save her, my heart soared being with Piers, though only for a moment.

I pause at a streetlight, barely aware of the turn of bulb from red to green. My body moves with the crowd as I drift and allow tiny trickles of flame to emerge, searching the city for him as I go. I don't dare let loose my power, not here, even if it might mean tracking him down, being able to spend time with him. Things have changed a great deal since our first meeting, though not as much as I'd like. Not his fault. Mine entirely. It's so hard to break the ingrained fear of outsiders, to share things that I've been told are for Oracles only. It's so tempting to reach out and find him, to let the flames burn and sizzle their way around Los Angeles until I feel his presence. But there are too many magic-gifted people in this city, and I've been taught well enough to keep my presence secret.

"Our family must never be revealed." How many times have I heard those words pass my grandmother's stern lips? "The Oracles of Helios must remain hidden from other magic races if our work is to be unbiased and clean of conscience."

My brow furrows, toe seeking out a small rock to kick into the street as I scowl at nothing. Why, then, the sorcerers, I wonder? Of course, I've never had the nerve to ask, not even when our quiet existence in the vast sanctuary under this city was taken over by a large group of young men, sorcerers all, and their arrogant and watchful leader eight years ago.

I take a break at a small café, sipping hot coffee from a small mug delivered by a smiling, stunningly beautiful barista. This city is full of women and men like her, come to chase a dream of fame and fortune in film and television. As her fingers brush mine, I catch a glimpse through flame of her, older, thinner, face marked and bruised, unconscious in a grungy bathroom with a needle in her arm. I jerk away, though she doesn't seem to notice, and sigh out a soft puff of smoke. Perhaps there is something I could do to help her, if I were permitted. And then again, perhaps not. The lives of normals seem so much more set in stone than those of other races, races with power, as though magic lends itself to flexible destiny.

My fingers drum on the sides of my cup as I people watch, giving up at last on seeing Piers this trip above. I try not to let the disappointment ruin my brief freedom. I have so little time before my grandmother comes looking for me and I don't want her to catch me with him.

That would be a disaster. While he's a sorcerer himself, I'm certain my stern and commanding matriarch would never understand my love for an outsider.

Cup of coffee done, I move on, the complexity of my life turning my mind, as it often does when I'm here, above ground and away from the influence of my family. My first meeting with Piers has led me deeper into doubt than I ever thought possible, and has only increased my anxiety. Not because of him specifically, or the werewoman, Charlotte, whose future I saw with such clarity I couldn't help but assist her. But because of the other face which has haunted me since I was very small.

I shudder despite the heat of the day when her blue eyes open in my mind. There was a time I thought I understood the reason for the visions, with her serious but beautiful face, her dark hair in a messy ponytail, the way everything about her pulsed with power.

FORESIGHT

My grandmother and her sorcerer mate both pounce on every single instance of vision that deals with her. And I long believed, because of their urgings and interpretation of my vision, this mystery woman was meant to bring about the end of the world. As a girl, I found it hard to accept, my innocent heart liking her on impulse. But who was I to question Sibyl, the woman who raised me, my own grandmother? For years I allowed no thoughts to the contrary. I glance sideways into the glass of a small shop, catching my reflection, my sad, dark eyes, hunched shoulders. Meeting Piers and Charlotte changed everything.

I slip my hands into the pockets of my cropped jacket, fingers encountering the silver lighter I've carried since I can remember. It was my mother's. The only thing I have left of her, and I cling to it as I turn another corner, head down another street, already lost to the sprawl of Los Angeles. My mind wanders elsewhere as my feet carry me into the deepening afternoon. It's never dark here, the street- and headlights shining over everything, illuminating the city as though it's just another kind of daylight. I slip my thumb over the cover of the smooth lighter and think of home.

I really need to go back. It's almost time for dinner and Sibyl will be looking for me. She's only caught me above twice, making it abundantly clear how disappointed she was to do so. And I don't relish her glare or coldness, or her veiled threats to confine me below. I've never taken such seriously, but I know better than to push her.

And yet, returning too soon means losing any chance I have of seeing Piers today. And if I go home now, Sibyl might find an excuse to sit me in the chapel and push me into foresight. It doesn't matter to her the things I see haven't changed much in several years. I'm just not in the mood to deal with her right now.

Regardless how many times I dissect and review the visions, I can't bring myself to believe the explanations handed to me by my family. Doubt clouds my mind as much as my heart, because something does not seem right.

It was hard to admit to myself, the night I first met Piers and his werewolf friend, Charlotte, that something was very wrong. Despite my deep-seated worries, carried with me all the days of my life, I didn't want to believe my family had been deceiving me. Other Oracles have seen what I have, if not as intensely or with such regularity. But we've all been told the same story for as long as I can remember: the woman with the blue eyes and the serious, lovely face is the enemy and we must guard against her.

Why, then, does her gaze seem so kind? Even when she's destroying the world in my visions, her expression is empathetic, broken with grief. I can't bring myself to trust the word of the family anymore, though I wish things were different. But I wouldn't rewind to that night and never meet Piers. He is my destiny, the other half of my heart.

And I've spent two years stealing brief moments with him.

A fire flickers to my right and I turn to stare into the joyful flames. Fire is my friend, the carrier of the visions, my traveling companion and constant warmth. I drift toward the underpass and the barrel of burning trash, staying out of the sight of those who gather around it. Homeless men and women cooking who knows what over the climbing flames. I see Piers's face in the fire, unbidden, hear his voice in my head, but it's just a memory, not a true vision. If it were, I wouldn't be aware of the rough concrete under my boots or the breeze pushing hair across my cheek.

I touch my lips with trembling fingers, feeling tears well. I've done my best to hide my doubt from the family, but with every day that passes, it grows more difficult and I feel rebellion grow. I'm tired of taking the word of my grandmother at the value she presents, the constant assurance I'm doing the right thing using my power to help her and the others plot to save us all. Because I fear, from what Piers has told me, they have been lying to me my entire life and now I don't know what to do about it.

I turn from the fire, kicking at a small stone, hearing it bounce across the street before I continue on. The flames beg me to return, but I resist. Along with the worry I'm being deceived, the pull of the fire has grown in the past two years. I can still control it, of course, but its call is a song in my heart, begging me to embrace it fully, something I can never do. I know it's a risk. There have been Oracles lost to the flames, devoured completely by the power that is meant to serve us. I am too strong to allow it to happen to me.

At least, I keep telling myself that's the case.

I reach the bottom of the street and slip into the shadows. This is a bad part of town, one I visit frequently, the exhilaration of visiting a dangerous place pushing back my fears about my life. I'm in no real peril. One flick of my lighter and I'm gone, traveling the flame back home, or anywhere else I'd like to go. But being here, where the sound of gunshots is as frequent as the call of sirens, I feel alive. Present.

Not some Oracle who is only good for viewing the future. But here, Zoe Helios, a person like any other, with meaning to her life outside the obvious.

Twenty-one years living for the flame and the visions has left little room for *me*. And the more I explore, probe, examine the things I've seen, the harder it is to resist the fire. But I must know the truth. My heart won't let me get this wrong.

I'm about to turn around when I feel him and everything stops. Ahead, he's there, I know it and the knowledge almost chokes me. I see him emerge from between two buildings, long, gray coat hanging to his feet, lean shoulders back, blond hair over one shoulder, falling in rippling silk to his knees. Those gray eyes greet me with joy, his lean hands already reaching out to me.

He turns, heads my way from the other side of the street. Coming closer. My lips are turning into a smile, my heart beginning to race, even as a mind touches mine.

Zoe. I close off immediately at the sound of Sibyl's cool curiosity. *Where are you?*

Coming, Grandmother. I panic, chest tightening around my sudden nerves. What do I think will happen if she finds out about Piers? I don't dare find out, just in case. She knows nothing of him or my visions of us together. I want it to stay that way.

I raise my hand to him, sorrowful and see him slow, stop. He nods, blows me a kiss. And lets me go.

I'll see you soon, he sends, his dark power embracing me a bare moment. I wish he hadn't. It makes leaving so much harder.

I jerk the lighter from my pocket, flipping open the lid. He doesn't make a sound, standing no more than ten feet away with his hands in the deep pockets of his coat. He watches with calm, adoring eyes and a small smile. One hand rises in farewell even as I strike the flame.

And dive into it, terrified my grandmother might take him away from me, after all.

TWO

It's Piers's face that keeps me focused and safe from the flames as I run for home. The fire licks at me, begs me to dance with it, to be part of it forever. I whisper love for it even as I slip free, the lid of my lighter snapping shut to gutter the pleading flame.

It's dark in the stone hall, a single lamp ahead lighting the way, though I don't need light to navigate this part of the sanctuary. It's been my home my entire life, and I know its walls, halls, and meeting places like I know my own soul.

—his lips meet yours, warm and soft, his breath sharp with peppermint. When he kisses you, your heart expands, so far, so fast you are certain you won't survive the need building in your chest. Strong hands grip you tight, your own winding in his silky hair, tongue invading his delicious mouth, one knee parting his legs,

stepping into him, pushing against him until you feel as one—

I snap out of the vision, panting for air, one hand impacting the wall beside me to keep from keeling over. I've frozen in position, lost completely to the future I've seen, cheeks flushed and body heated from the experience.

Thank Gaia no one is in this part of the sanctuary. I've avoided being embarrassed by my steamy future. Piers and I have, as yet, to connect this way, so I know it's pending. Our brief, stolen moments together are so few and far between, spent wandering the city together or just talking, I wonder when we will ever find the chance. There is nothing shy about him, so perhaps it's me he's waiting for.

And I confess, I'm not ready to give anyone my heart, not until I know for sure whose side I'm really on.

I need to stop wasting time. Sibyl's attention has moved on, gone elsewhere, so at least there's that small miracle. She's notorious for checking in with me from time to time, at the oddest moments. I can't help but think she's stalking me. I'm just grateful I learned long ago how to mask my position, to bring with me through my power the feeling of the sanctuary so she would only know the difference if she actually came to find me.

The first time I snuck above was the first time I learned that lesson and I've only slipped up once since.

My feet carry me forward as I finally discard the last

of my reticence, though a tiny jolt of nerves worms its way through me. I've gone too long pretending at finding answers. This future I just visioned, it's close, very close, the intensity telling me my time with Piers could happen soon. Which means if I'm to follow through, as I know I will, I must have some resolution to my divided mind.

Head down, I march for my room, winding my decision over in my head, though I know it's the right one. I can choose to continue feeling conflicted, letting doubt tear me apart. Or, I can dig for answers and uncover the truth behind what I'm seeing.

If this blue-eyed woman truly is the Light One and not the Dark as I've been told, I need to understand why we are so misguided and who, exactly, is the real enemy.

I almost feel better as I take the short flight of steps to the next level and the living quarters. I pass a pair of young girls who giggle behind their hands, soft cream robes whispering around their feet as they skip on. I owe it to them, to the Oracles of my family, to find out why we are being misled, or, if we aren't, to clear my mind at long last.

I'm so deep in my contemplations, I miss the fact someone waits by my room. When I finally realize I'm not alone, it's too late to slow my pace, too late to avoid the grinning, handsome young man leaning against my doorframe.

A soft groan tries to rise, but I smother it with a

forced smile of my own, turning sideways to Kayden as I unlock my door with a touch of flame.

His hand brushes my hair and I twitch away, the lock making a soft sound under my touch. "Looking beautiful, as usual," he says. His voice is a warm tenor, full of meaning and song, and is sighed over by some of the younger girls. They can have him. That angel's tone disguises a dark core, needy and hurtful. I've seen him destroy more than one Oracle's heart with a careless glee that leaves me with a vile taste in my mouth.

I open the door, but only a crack, staring up at him with my blankest expression. Anger does nothing, kindness is worse. The only response that seems to frustrate him is empty nothingness. "Excuse me," I say.

His green eyes flicker with anger, but he's still smiling, one hand falling on my upper arm. It's not an overt move, but I know if I try to pull away, he'll tighten his grip. How Kayden loves the chase. I refuse to become a toy for his pleasure.

"Dinner awaits." He gestures with his free hand, straightening to his full height, a head over me. His dark blond hair spikes artfully, chest broad under an expensive shirt. He's spent hours in front of the mirror, I can only guess, as self-absorbed as he is arrogant. "Thought you'd join me tonight." White teeth flash as the touch of his dark magic makes its way from the floor at his feet to pool under mine.

My flames react before I think, burning away the black tendrils of sorcery before they can advance any further. He hisses at me, squeezing my arm, but flames erupt there, too, and he pulls back, shaking his singed hand.

I see the fury in his eyes, the monster of hate he hides from everyone, pass through his gaze and know he will hurt me if he can. My fire rises from the depths of me, ready to act, flames disturbing my view of him as they burn in my eyes.

"Zoe!" I spin at the sound of my name, Kayden's hand grasping once again, squeezing hard enough to leave a bruise before dropping away. Dark hair bobs around full cheeks as my cousin, Rena, comes to a halt next to me, bright smile turning up toward Kayden. Her full breasts strain against her t-shirt as she turns her head and winks at him with blown kiss. "Hello there, handsome."

Kayden is all charm again, leaning past me to kiss Rena's hand. She giggles when he releases her, smiling like nothing just happened between us.

"I'll see you two at dinner, I guess." He doesn't look at me, sauntering off with his ass stuffed into tight jeans, long legs carrying him in smooth strides down the hall to the stairs. Rena sighs audibly, leaning against the wall next to my door, fanning herself.

"That," she says, "is the definition of hotness."

I roll my eyes, pushing open my door. "I prefer

flames," I say.

She follows me into my quarters, flopping down into the large sofa next to the fireplace. I shed my jacket, draping it over a chair, before heading to my bedroom and the bathroom attached to it.

"Where have you been?" Rena's high voice sounds petulant, though I know she's only teasing me. "I've been looking everywhere for you."

"Walking the deep halls," I say, crossing my room to the bathroom door. The light switch rewards me with a reflection in the mirror, my tired face still angry. I need to learn not to wear my emotions so clearly, and am usually much better at it. But Kayden and his dual nature bring out the worst in me.

"Whatever for?" Rena appears at the bathroom door as I twist my long, dark hair into a bun at the base of my neck. She wrinkles her small nose. "You spend far too much time alone."

I turn to meet her brown eyes, as dark as my own, though that and our thick, black hair are the only two traits we share. She has her father's build, the sorcerer who mated with her mother a stocky man with round cheeks and thick limbs. My father was tall, from what I've been told, and lean, like Piers.

I must not think of Piers. My cheeks heat as I turn from Rena's watchful gaze, to splash water on my face in the hope of cooling the sudden burst of flame rising when I think of him.

"Helps the visions," I say, hoping she'll drop it.

She does, though when she speaks again, I almost sigh and wish she'd go back to her previous line of questioning.

"Rumor is, Kayden asked Sibyl to be your Pyros." Rena sounds like she's jealous, but I couldn't care less for her hurt feelings as I gasp and turn to her again, water still dripping down my face. She hands me a towel with an irritated expression. "Oh, for Gaia's sake, Zoe. Surely you knew it was coming. You're twenty-one, already two years past choosing a partner. And Kayden is the most eligible of all the sorcerers."

I shrug, patting at my face to cover my disgust. "Considering there are so many of them, and so few of us, I plan to take my time choosing." Rena can't argue with my logic. Nor can my grandmother, though Sibyl has tried. I suppress a sigh as I think about it. Over a hundred young sorcerers live in the sanctuary, all men hoping for one of the dozen or so Oracle women of mating age to choose them. There are times I feel like I'm living in a game show and I'm the prize.

Rena hooks my arm in hers, all smiles. "Then let's go examine a few and see who fits the bill." She throws me a saucy wink, leading me out of my room and down the hall, barely giving me time to lock my door.

It's hard not to laugh at her antics as she flirts with

the first pair of young sorcerers we encounter, flashing her busty chest and wiggling her walk as we pass them. She's only seventeen, still two years from mating, but I can tell she'll have no problem deciding who she wants to claim as a partner, though maybe it will be an issue for Rena. Not that multiple partners are frowned on, but she might wear herself out.

I snicker at the thought and Rena grins at me, clearly thinking I'm into her little game.

"At least this batch is cute," she says, whispering to me as we descend into the main level and our encounters with others grow more frequent. I avoid eye contact with the black-clothed sorcerers, as much as I take time to smile and wave to the cream-clad Oracles who are my family.

"Time was we could choose from any normal men," I say, hearing the complaint in my voice, knowing it stems from thinking of Piers followed by Kayden's assault. From the tenderness of my arm, I know he's left a dark bruise with his heavy handedness.

"I think it's a great idea," Rena says, snotty nature showing. "No more hiding who we are from our suitors. No more worry our normal mates might betray us." And what of the sorcerers? I wonder. She goes on, oblivious. "And no more running a risk of having a talentless and unseeing baby." Rena shudders. "Imagine." She's always been more than a little pompous about our position, though I find nothing to be arrogant about. We have a sacred gift, given to us by our beloved Gaia. Feeling superior about it seems disrespectful to the Goddess. "And considering it was Grandmother's idea?"

Sibyl's plans for us seem promising. How many times have I heard her tell us tying our fate to the sorcerers only makes us stronger?

I'm not so sure, especially now, though Piers himself is a sorcerer. I lick my lips as we pass through the arched opening and into the dining hall, the pressure of sound almost sending me back out again. The weight of the presence of so many people, the volume of their voices and the closeness feels like an invasion every single time.

Only a hundred and fifty or so souls, but enough to pull me to a halt with my heart in my throat. Being around so many people can trigger my visions, especially the family. And sorcery seems to feed the flames, rather than the other way around.

Rena pulls on my arm, keeping me moving, while my tension slowly eases. No visions, at least, not yet. I sink into the seat she pulls out for me with impatience before landing hard in her own next to me with a gusty sigh of irritation.

"For Gaia's sake, Zoe," Rena rolls her eyes at me. "We don't bite."

She's never experienced the level of connection I have to the future so I hold back an angry retort. Instead,

I look up, and find my grandmother watching me.

Sibyl waves, like a queen on her throne, dark hair gone steel gray, though her face is as young as any woman here. Her deep brown eyes observe me, making me squirm under such scrutiny.

How was your walk, dear? She smiles ever so slightly.

Fine, thank you. I try to look away, but her mind holds me, her fire that of old coals and heat.

Anything new to report? She's heard the same excuse I gave Rena, that walking the halls helps me with my foresight. It seems to keep her placated enough she doesn't hunt me down every time I disappear.

Not today. I very firmly cut her off, though I know I'll pay for it later. But I can't have her in my head right now. Haven't I just decided to prove she's been lying to me? Being in her presence makes me feel like small, as it always does, though I surpassed her own power at visioning long ago.

Her partner sits beside her, face tight as he devours his meal. I look away quickly so I don't have to meet his sharp gaze, the way his goatee hugs his thin mouth always stirring feelings of unease. Perhaps it's because he's a small man he works so hard to appear larger than life. But the result simply raises the hairs on the backs of my arms. It doesn't help he and Sibyl are always preaching preparedness, stirring fear. I look around the room, at the eager young sorcerers, the Oracles of my family. I hope

21

I'm wrong, though I know now, more than ever, I'm right about being lied to.

Something is coming, all right. Liander Belaisle is correct about that. But the cause and the future are far different than I think he and my grandmother are willing to admit.

"Rena." I look down at the plate of steaming vegetables and the slice of rare meat before me, the scent suddenly making me ill. "Do you ever doubt what you see?"

She stares at me like I've grown a second head. "You've been so odd lately," she huffs, filling her mouth with mashed potatoes, washing it down with water. "Are you all right, Zoe?"

I shrug, hands tight in my lap. "It's nothing."

Her hand reaches for mine, covering them with her pudgy little fingers. But her intense gaze is caring, not judging as she speaks.

"I'm worried," she whispers. "You've been too much in the flame."

I pull free of her, smile, shake my head. "I'm fine, I promise." I sigh and lift my fork, prodding my dinner. "Just not hungry."

Rena nabs my plate with a wink. "Can't let it go to waste."

I sit in silence in a room filled with sound and wonder if she's right about me. While I think of Piers and hope.

THREE

I swirl the water around in my crystal glass, keeping my head down while Rena chatters away beside me, overflowing the space between us with her endless runoff. I nod politely from time to time, grunting agreement here and there, all she needs to continue.

A flicker of motion on my left draws my gaze, lifts my chin enough I can observe who hides in wait. I'm not surprised to spot Rupe hunched in the doorway leading to the main hall of the sanctuary. He always seems to hover, on the outside looking in, his face twisted in a mixed look of madness and terrible loss. Big hands flutter at his sides, pattering over the dirty fabric of his jeans, his t-shirt stained and hanging in baggy dejection from his shoulders.

His eyes catch mine, head jerking around as though

he knows I'm watching him and, for a moment, I fear he's noticed me. I have nothing to be afraid of. Rupe is Liander's pet, well- heeled and knows full well if he were to harm any of us, his sorcerous master would punish him. And has in the past when Rupe's eager insanity has led him to strike out at one of the sorcerers living in the sanctuary. But there is such hopelessness in the man's eyes, such a lack of reason and so much despair I wonder if perhaps, someday, Liander might lose control of the beast living inside the young sorcerer and, in doing so, let loose such rage as we have never seen.

For he is a sorcerer. I feel the darkness in him, my Oracle's power set deep in the black of that base magic. But he also has fire inside, and a creature I can't identify. At times I sense the same from him as I did with Charlotte, the werewolf woman. But his beast doesn't have the calm quiet of lupine possession. If Rupe is, in fact, part werewolf, something has gone terribly wrong with his assimilation.

Rupe waves at me with sudden enthusiasm and I remember the person he used to be, an image of a tall, strong-willed and handsome man superimposed over the hunched wreck he's become.

"That ghastly piece of work really needs to find somewhere to curl up and die." Rena rolls her eyes, jabbing the air between her and Rupe with her silver fork. "Honestly, he acts like he's still king of this castle or something, instead of a waste of space."

My forehead creases into a frown before I can stop myself, nodding to a young woman who bows to me before taking away my unused cutlery. She has a little power, but is mostly latent, like all the servants who care for the sanctuary. I wonder how difficult it must be for her, surrounded by so much magic and only able to access a fraction of her own. If it were me, I'm not sure if I'd rather avoid the powered, save myself the pain of lack, or be immersed in the hope maybe, one day, my own would wake.

I don't have to worry about such things, but my empathy is more powerful than I am at times. Like now. I study Rupe as he slides further back into shadow, eyes locked on Liander and Sibyl. It's hard not to pity him, at least for me.

"I used to think he was so handsome." Rena sets down her fork as the same young servant takes her plate, waving the girl off with absent arrogance. "You remember?"

I do. I nod in answer, heart seeping a little for Rupe as he shakes his head, tapping his temple with one finger, whispering to himself. Surely Liander could see fit to either heal Rupe or somehow ease his pain?

Rena's eyes narrow as she turns to me. "Tell me you don't feel sorry for him."

I roll my shoulders, sipping my water for a

distraction. "He's mad," I say. "There's no need to prolong his suffering."

"Liander seems to think so." Rena sniffs at my reluctance to agree.

Something cracks inside me, anger sizzling in fire through the crumbling ashes of my sadness. "Your precious Liander isn't all that anymore himself." I catch my breath, cursing softly at myself in my head. I never meant to speak that out loud.

Rena winks at me, a wicked grin on her lips. Seems she doesn't care whom she gossips about, as long as she gets the chance to be spiteful. "I know, right?" She casts a slow glance at the end of the table where our grandmother murmurs a conversation with the sorcerer leader. "I remember being so scared of him when we were little." She twiddles her fingers at me, sparks falling from them to the table while I hiss at her and bat them out.

Something changed in him, we all felt it. Eight years ago, things were different. Liander's visits were infrequent, though often enough to keep my grandmother happy. And then, he appeared one night and hasn't left since, at least not for any length of time. Shortly thereafter, his young sorcerers began to appear and the new arrangements with his people and mine began.

"I hear he's lost most of his power." Rena taps the

side of my glass with one manicured nail, cheeks rosy with the joy of her secret offering. "That he's hiding here."

I chew my lower lip, not meaning to stare at him but my eyes drawn to his face as she speaks.

The Liander I remember as a girl was arrogant and self-assured. The one who dominates the sanctuary now is bitter, cruel.

"I don't get his reasoning," Rena says, accepting a large slice of chocolate cake from the serving girl. I wave mine off, only to have my cousin grab the girl's arm and pull her back. "Why he had us stop our readings is beyond me."

She's as bad as some of the older Oracles, gossiping so. And I have no doubt her emulation of them is intentional. Her own mother is the queen of controversy, something I do my best to steer clear of.

Rena is correct, though. I remember as a little girl, being asked to read for outsiders, brought to expensive mansions and sea-side houses, penthouse suites and underground offices, all to see the future for private, wealthy clients of the Oracles.

Liander's permanent residence put an end to that. Now, we only read for him. I've often wondered why the change. It feels as though we've lost our purpose, though Liander insists—as does my grandmother—our future depends on our secrecy.

"We should be out there," I mutter. "Helping like we used to."

Rena pokes me with the tines of her fork. "I, for one, prefer not playing trick pony," she says, her arrogance returned. She licks chunks of cake from her knuckles. "Besides, we shouldn't be talking about this."

Leave it to my blabbermouth cousin to tell me I'm speaking out of turn.

Rena is suddenly waving at someone across the table. I look up, startled, to find Sibyl watching us. Our grandmother nods to me and I nod back before ducking my head again, holding her mind at bay, a little surprised she doesn't force the issue. I don't want to talk to her right now. There are times I feel she can see right through me and this isn't a time I'd like to be proven right.

Rena hisses a moment later, setting down her fork even as I feel them approach. I turn slowly, plastering a smile on my face, and stand to greet my grandmother.

She kisses my cheek with her cool lips.

When she turns to greet Rena in the same fashion, Liander takes her place beside me. He's smiling as well, but there is animosity in his eyes and I can't shake the feeling he knows he gives me the creeps.

"Liander!" Rena practically falls over her own feet to reach his side, bubbling with her usual need to be noticed. Never mind she was just speaking ill of him only a moment ago. "So kind of you to come to say hello tonight."

He ignores her, gaze locked on mine as he closes the distance between us by simply swaying forward. I feel his power push against me and allow it, knowing if I resist he'll dig deeper. Let him feel the surface all he wants. I know better than to face off against him. Yes, I'm certain I could defeat him if the matter came to such a conflict, but it's not worth challenging him when my grandmother is watching with her cold gaze.

"Zoe." Liander's voice sends goosebumps down my arms. He must be half snake. "Your grandmother and I would see you in our chambers later."

I can't think of something I'd rather not do, but I nod instead of rebelling.

He turns without a word, Sibyl taking his arm even as he strides off. Rena glares up at me a moment before shrugging off her jealousy.

"Thinks he's all that," she says.

FOUR

I turn to leave, only to have Rena grab my arm. Her fingernails dig in, and I can tell before I meet her eyes, she's angry with me. I sigh and grasp her hand, pulling her after me, toward my room. She walks with heavy steps, pouting, while I lead her up the stairs, down the hall and through my door.

Rena doesn't come inside, though I release her before entering. I turn to gesture to her to join me, heart sore, knowing why she's angry and unable to do anything about it.

"Please," I say. She's my closest friend and it's time this thing between us went away. "Rena, talk to me."

She flounces her way in, pulling the door sharply shut

behind her. I join her on the couch as she sags into it, eyes tight and frustrated.

"It's not fair." She looks away from me, sniffling a little. I have to remind myself she's only seventeen, four years younger than me. Was I so childish only a few short years ago? "It's all about you, every time." She makes a bitter face. "'Zoe, you're so powerful.' 'Zoe, you're so talented.'" Rena stands and storms over to the fireplace where only coals remain. "There are other Oracles in this Gaia forsaken place who have visions."

I stay where I am, hands folded in my lap. "You are very powerful," I say, though it's partially a lie. Rena has ability, but she is too lazy to hone it. I hide a wince at my harsh but private assessment as she turns and smiles at me, a flash of thanks.

"I know you're special," she says, voice soft. "But we all are."

This time I stand and go to her, hugging her. She hugs me back, cheek on my shoulder.

"We are," I say. "The most special every created, the daughters of Gaia, the earth mother. Thanks to her, we have the power to see into the future."

"Some of us better than others." Rena pulls away, wiping at her cheeks with her hands and I only then realize she's been crying.

I grip her shoulders in my hands and shake her ever so gently. "I would trade places with you, my dear cousin, if I could."

She smiles again before offering one of her trademark eye rolls. "Sure you would." She flicks her fingers at my shirt sleeve, twisting her torso back and forth, looking up through her lashes, her sadness gone. "Thanks, Zoe."

I let her go then, waving goodbye at my door, firmly locking it behind me when she's gone. I take a step toward my bedroom—

—You look out over the city, see it burning and know she is the cause. Her face hovers behind the flame-engulfed towers, see her scowl as they scream in the streets, dying, desperate while she raises her arms over her head and her rainbow flames engulf everything—

I know this vision, so when I stagger free of it, I'm not as disoriented as I could be. I've seen it many times before, though it's the first time I've seen the city on fire before she appeared. I hurry across my living room and into my bedroom, hands already out and reaching for my jacket and the lighter inside. It's cold in my palm for a moment, quickly warming to my skin temperature as I weigh it in my hand.

This requires investigating, I think. But not here. I need the extra focus I can gain from the chapel. I slip into my jacket, lighter in hand, and head out, locking my door behind me.

The halls are quiet this time of night, everyone settling in after dinner. It's easy to avoid others as I make my way downstairs and past the dining hall, trailing a moment behind a pair of young sorcerers before losing them as I duck into a side corridor.

The main chapel doors are open, as usual, though the altar and its cover stone remains closed. A single touch of flame lights the candles at the base of the dais, and I settle into the hard, stone bench where Oracles have sat for generations before me.

It's quiet here without my family filling the first two rows, the push of black power from the sorcerers who fill the rest. I prefer the cool silence hovering over the room, the way it feels holy, as though I am in the presence of something much bigger than me.

I am, of course, though she is hidden under stone. I feel Gaia here the most powerfully, the connection to my Goddess and the flames so strong I'm sure, given enough time, I could see everything that could ever happen until the end of life itself.

Tonight, I'm only focused on what I've seen. I flick open my lighter and wake the flame with a spin of the wheel—

—*Her, the Dark/Light One, the Werewolf, the Sorcerer, all of them, as clear as though they stand next to you. A house, white, black shutters, with a big yard, and a deep green fire burning under the ground. A dragon in the guise of a man, his diamond eyes seeing right through you, a fearful fount of flame rushing toward you as she charges on his back.*

A giant battle, but in the past, a hundred dragons, Liander full of power, towering over the Dark/Light One, the dragons falling to the ground, brought low by his magic. He is the hero, or so you've been told, and yet your heart mourns for the great beasts who lie helpless at the foot of a massive stronghold.

You never see the end of the battle, though you feel it ends badly for the one who you serve. She was the victor, you are certain. But it doesn't matter, not when another war unfolds, creatures of shining, iridescent magic attacking others of their kind, Dark against Light, while the dragon creatures circle and observe.

She is there, her rainbow power flaring into flames, her arms raising, engulfing everything in a flash of multi-colored fire—

I gasp a breath as I leave the vision, though not the fire. It begs me to stay, embraces me with its heat and I fall into it a moment, the searing temperature making me cry out. The flame on my lighter splutters and goes out, jerking me free of the seeking fire. I lower my shaking hand, muscles aching from holding it rigid for so long, and hang my head. Beads of sweat form on my upper lip, my tongue swiping over them, the salty heat tinged with the taste of soot.

The lighter drops into my lap as I slide my hands over my face and look down at them. Black dust clings to my sweating fingers. I've never gone so far into the fire before, stayed so long. If my lighter's flame hadn't died...

I might have.

But if that's the case, why did it feel so good to embrace the fire?

My palms rub over the tops of my thighs, transferring the soot to my jeans. Enough for now, but I know more than I did. I used to only see the final scene, where the one Charlotte called Syd raised her arms, rainbow power devouring everything and came to believe—thanks to Sibyl and Liander—it meant she would be the cause of the end of the Universe.

Now I'm not so sure. The battle of the magic warriors makes me wonder. I still don't have all the pieces. But I can't risk going back into the flame tonight. I shudder at the thought, now I'm out of it. It's just too dangerous.

My knees shake as I stand and turn to leave the chapel, mind in my visions as I absently snuff the candles behind me with a touch of power. And realize, too late, I'm not alone.

FIVE

I exhale in surprise, though I'm smiling by the time the last of the air leaves my lungs and stepping forward, arms outstretched. The pair of Oracle siblings before me grin in turn and come to hug me all at once, a three person embrace I cling to as they whisper their greetings in my ears.

I'm surprised to find tears standing in my eyes as I pull away, and cover my emotional reaction to seeing them with a laugh. The only male born of our family with Oracle powers, Thanos grins at me, arms dropping to his sides, though his eyes don't see me. Both he and his sister were born blind, milky white orbs creating a stir every time they appear in the sanctuary. Though I never once thought them disturbing. Instead, I greatly enjoy their calm and confident manner, the way neither of them seem anxious about the past or nervous about the future, living in the present as true Oracles should.

"We thought to find you here," Thanos says with humor in his voice.

"Where else, if not the streets of the city above?" His sister, Bellanca, smiles at me, hand reaching for mine. I always have the impression these two can see more with their other senses than I can with my eyes alone. Her aim is unerring, as usual, fingers catching mine.

I follow them to a bench and sit, looking forward to the altar, Thanos on one side, Bellanca on the other, happy to be sandwiched between them. Rena might be my closest friend here in the sanctuary, but the Helios twins are siblings of my heart.

"How long are you back?" They are of the few number of our order who live outside the sanctuary, often off on missions for Sibyl. Though blind, I've never doubted their capability in handling whatever my grandmother intends for them. They radiate such confidence I wish it would rub off on me.

"Always with the questions," Thanos says, tilting his head toward me so the light from above catches the bristly blonde of his close-shaven hair.

I shoulder bump him. "Sorry," I say. "I guess I'm just feeling a little lonely these days." Should I tell them of

Piers? Of all the Oracles in my family, I feel these two would understand, not only about my obsession with the outsider sorcerer, but my worries about my visions and the interpretations I've been taught to believe.

"Poor darling." Bellanca raises my hand to her lips and kisses the back of it. "We hate to abandon you so frequently."

"Duty calls." Thanos sounds as sad as his sister, and I feel instantly guilty.

"You're here now," I say, forcing brightness into my tone. "Tell me everything you've been doing."

"Better yet." Thanos turns sideways, one arm draped over the bench back, face serious. "Tell us what you've been doing."

I stammer a moment, suddenly nervous, though not because of them. More of voicing the truth of what I've been feeling. But in that moment, sitting in Gaia's chapel with my dear friends beside me, I know it's time to finally share my concerns.

My words tumble from my mouth like falling tears as I confess my deepest fears to them. Neither of the twins speak as I talk of my meeting with Charlotte and Piers two years ago, or of the doubtful seeds the werewoman planted. Of my secret meetings with the young sorcerer, though I don't tell them of how deeply I feel for him or that I've been visioning him for years.

Of course, they both know exactly who I refer to

when I speak of the Dark One, but neither shows a flicker of surprise when I tell them Charlotte claims the woman of my visions is, in fact, the exact opposite. She is, instead, the savior of our Universe. I barely whisper the words, feeling as though I've committed some great sacrilege, doubting Gaia's gift in her own chapel. But once I begin, I can't stop, completing my verbal spill with what I've just seen.

Hot tears drop to my lap as I finish, throat tight with guilt. Bellanca's fingers still grip my hand, Thanos's falling on my shoulder as he leans forward and presses his lips to my temple.

"So brave," his sister whispers. "Dear Zoe."

"You believe me?" I choke on those words, unable to convince myself they aren't about to leap up and run for Sibyl, to name me a traitor and have me imprisoned. I'm shaking all over, teeth chattering, as Bellanca turns her blind eyes to me with a sad smile.

"We've known all along," she says, surprising me so much my tears dry up in an instant. "But you had to uncover the truth for yourself."

I'd be angry, except she's right. Any attempt at fury dies as I nod, accepting her words. This isn't something one can be told—that an entire existence is a lie, a manipulation. It's a truth that must be experienced.

"What do I do?" I look back and forth between them.

Thanos sighs softly, his breath ruffling my hair.

"What do you want to do?"

"I need to talk to Grandmother." Surely Sibyl has no idea. Which awakens my anger, and this time it lives on without being snuffed out by reason. "Liander Belaisle. He must be the source of the deception." I can't bring myself to believe my grandmother would agree to such, so she has to be warned. I look back and forth between the twins, a small hope in my heart. If they know… "Will you come with me? To tell her?"

Neither responds positively, or at all for that matter, and my tiny seed of maybe dies.

Bellanca shifts beside me, face pensive. "Perhaps it is Liander Belaisle who you must guard against," she says. "Though things are often more complicated than we want to accept." She tilts her head to one side, braid falling over her shoulder to pool in her lap. "If anyone can find the true path, Zoe, it's you."

I open my mouth to ask her what she means. The twins are often cryptic when we talk, never quite answering questions when asked directly. But Thanos speaks up, silencing me.

"A time is coming, Zoe," he says, voice deepening, power rumbling through him. I can feel his fire waking as he goes on. "A time when you will be forced to make a choice."

I shake my head, not in denial but in wonder. "I don't understand."

The pair rises, Thanos brushing past me to join his sister. Her hand gestures, flames rising from her fingertips.

"Know you are on the right path," Bellanca says while Thanos frowns at her like she's overstepped her bounds. "Trust your heart, Zoe."

Thanos grasps his sister's hand, the fire leaping as the two disappear into it. Leaving me with more questions than I had before, and the odd sense I'm missing an important piece of the puzzles that are Bellanca and Thanos.

SIX

I wake to the sound of bells and curse softly to myself as I scramble from the bed. I don't have time to shower, last night's clothes stripped from my body as I jerk open the door to my wardrobe and pull out my ceremony robe. The heavy red fabric falls to my feet, brushing my bare toes, hood hanging over my shoulders as a niggling thought crosses my mind, like a flame just blown out, a wisp of smoke remaining. Have I forgotten something? It feels as though I have, though what exactly escapes me. I wrestle a brush and my thick hair, finally managing a rough bun at the base of my neck, sandals sliding into place, even as I run for the door and decide if it's important enough, whatever I've forgotten will come to me eventually.

I must have been more tired than I thought last night

when I finally made it home to my quarters, because I have little recollection of falling onto my bed and passing out. A dreamless sleep did much to revive me, though I'm now, as I hurry through the hall toward the central worship hall, remembering the troubling conversation I had with the twins.

Relief is welcome after all my anxiety over the matter. At least now I know I'm not the only one with suspicions. I have a pair of allies. I think. Now I reflect on it, was Bellanca more on my side than Thanos?

I can't allow myself to divide them in my mind. They are my friends, my family. I trust them more than anyone in this world. If they believe me—have known all along as they claim—I can believe them, in turn.

Which makes my stomach sink as I slip past three girls in red robes, brushing by a knot of sorcerers grumbling about the early hour and stupid ceremony, sandals sliding over the stone floor as I take my breathless place in the second row behind the elder Oracles—the exact same seat I warmed last night—just as the last bell sounds.

Rena glares at me, poking my ribs. "You're late," she hisses in my ear.

I stick my tongue out at her, a childish gesture. "I'm here, aren't I?"

And then there's no more time for talk. The worship hall is full, the first two rows lined with red robes, the back stacked with black. I miss the quiet of the space, long for the empty silence that embraced me only hours ago in this sacred place. Well trained, we rise as one in a whisper of velvet and satin to greet the pair who mount the central dais, hand in hand.

My grandmother's red robe is trimmed in gold, Liander's black one in silver. Both wear elaborate headdresses, towering over them like steeples of a human church. Sibyl gestures with her free hand and the casing of the dais opens to the chorus of many sighs.

This was the only thing missing from my experience last night, the single regret I have when I come to chapel alone. Without Sibyl and Liander, I have no access to the blessed one below the stone slab. I ease toward the aisle, eyes locked on the shining rainbow case and the recumbent figure inside. Just the sight of my Goddess makes everything better, brighter. I forget for a moment my fears and anxieties, the warning from the twins, my two years of struggle with doubt. Being in the presence of Gaia always gives me peace.

She is so beautiful lying there in a cloth of pure white, face peaceful, hands folded over her generous breast. I've loved her since the first time I saw her as a tiny girl, my heart lost to my Goddess forever. The rainbow light surrounding her hums softly to me, a welcoming song I long to learn, though when she's again returned to the safety of her vault in her gold gilt bed, I forget it immediately. The loss makes my heart ache.

A clump of black mars my view and I look up with irritation to find Liander staring down at Gaia with a gaze of pure possession. My stomach clenches against the need to hit him with fire, to knock him back away from my Goddess. Like she needs my protection. And yet, I can't help but hate him with a passion that shocks me for looking at her like that.

She's his only focus these days, it seems. And though it was Liander who brought her to us, who made our Goddess manifest, I still wish him ill for his attention.

My eyes return to her, and I'm lost in her song again. It is my honor to serve, as the Oracles of Delphi—the first beloved of Gaia—once did so long ago. Love like I feel only when I look upon her floods my entire body, adoration for the Goddess who watches over us and protects us, who supplies the power of my family and the sorcerers we partner. Who grants us the foresight to know what's coming, to protect the world from chaos.

On impulse, without thinking or considering what my action might mean, for the first time in my life I reach out to Gaia directly and send her my love.

And feel her stir at my touch.

I retreat immediately, in shock and fear of what I might have done, even as the ceremony goes on without me. There seem to be no ill effects, though I feel at any moment fire and destruction will bring the sanctuary low.

That I've caused some great damage by my audacity. But no one seems to notice what I've done. Sibyl and Liander go about the morning ritual as though nothing happened.

Still, I'm shaking with nerves by the time the service ends and don't wait for the normal exodus line, slipping from my seat and hurrying to the exit before the first row can rise.

I find a quiet corner and pant out my stress, hand clutched to my chest, body tucked in shadows as the rest of the congregation files out, chatting and ignoring me while the panic inside me finally stills.

What was I thinking? I know better. No one is to touch Gaia with power. She is a Goddess, in perfect balance. Any interference with her balance can raise her ire. Clearly, I wasn't thinking. I've completely lost my mind.

And yet, as I finally leave the cubby's shadows and hurry toward my rooms, I catch myself frowning and thinking too hard. I touched Gaia with power. And she answered me. But not with anger or with punishment.

Why, now that I'm aware enough to examine the experience, did it feel like she was asleep?

SEVEN

I'm so absorbed in my thoughts, I miss the fact I have a visitor at my door, though when I look up I'm hardly surprised to find Kayden standing there yet again. He looks impatient before he spots me, charming smile smothering his true irritation as I slow my steps with a sigh heaved in his direction.

He's the last person I want to deal with right now. Why can't he just take the hint and leave me alone?

I'm accustomed to Kayden's typical attitude, the way he tries to touch me in seemingly innocent ways, how his hands tend to roam if he thinks he can get away with it. But when I stop at my door to unlock it, I'm not prepared for this more aggressive young sorcerer who maneuvers his body around me, blocking me between the heavy wood and the corridor. Both of his hands settle, palm down, on the stone frame of my doorway, head bowing over mine as he invades my space with his body and his power.

I'm so shocked by this sudden assault, I simply gape up at him as he grins, eyes sparking with something I can only call hunger.

"You and I need to have a serious conversation." There's a sultry tone to his voice I'm sure most of the other young Oracles would swoon over, but the way he speaks to me, how his sorcery slips over me like an oil slick, makes me want to throw up. "About our future together."

My anger recoils inside me before surging forward as my hands rise unbidden and slam against his chest. He steps back a pace, nostrils flaring, showing his own temper, as I clench my fingers around their trembling and face him down. Flames rise at my feet, dancing over the stones in answer to his unwelcome attention.

"I've been nice to you," I say, a little shocked at my bluntness, more used to taking the soft approach. But it seems he only understands forthrightness and anger. "I've been patient with you." The fire beneath me rises in time with my words, the scent of burning fabric reaching me. I let out a whisper of sorcery to devour the flames trying to set my robe on fire, while letting the surface ones live as a warning to Kayden. He looks down at them with a hint of nerves before meeting my eyes again. "But I'm done. It's time you understand, without question, we have no future." I snap my fingers in front of his eyes, show him the two of us, older, separate. No, it's not a true vision, just an illusion I've created, but hopefully it will do the trick. "You'd be best served finding an Oracle willing to pair with you," I say, allowing the fire to die though it takes some effort to hide my trembling from the rise in adrenaline. I hate confrontations. "This Oracle isn't interested."

Kayden's face sinks into bitterness and anger and I realize in the long, frightening moment he remains silent, staring, I've only made things worse by rejecting him.

A bulky figure crashes into Kayden just as the young sorcerer is about to strike out at me. Startled, I press my back against my door, fingers fumbling for flame to unlock it, while Kayden struggles a few feet away to regain his balance. I stare at Rupe, who twirls away from his attack with a big, dopey grin on his face. He tips a non-existent hat to me while Kayden roars in fury.

Rupe's eyes widen and he turns, scuttling off with Kayden on his heels as I watch, panting softly through my parted lips. Rupe is known for his crazy antics, his taunting of the young sorcerers and general madness. But it seems highly coincidental he would interrupt at exactly the moment I needed rescuing most. I shudder as I turn and push my door open, slipping inside. The wood is cool against my forehead as I lean against it, closing my eyes.

I've always treated the insane half-wolf sorcerer with respect, if not kindness and pity. Perhaps, somewhere deep in his cracked mind, he acted from his lost humanity.

Or, more likely, he saw an opportunity to cause havoc and took it. I shake my head, turning toward my bedroom, hands pulling at my robe. I know better than to assign compassion to others. I've been too often disappointed.

A knock summons me back before I'm able to shed my robe. I hesitate as I approach, but only a moment. The magic on the other side is as bright and hot as mine and I recognize the touch of my aunt even before I turn the handle and open the door.

She grins at me, blonde hair tousled, eyes half-lidded, beautiful face tired and a little worse for wear in the makeup department. I reach for her, pull her inside, Aunt Ash embracing me in a wash of old alcohol and what smells like last night's weed. No matter she's come to see me from another of her all-night benders, I'm happy to see her.

Her strong hands push me away, saucy grin on her face. "Zo," she says. "You look like crap."

I slap her arm with a laugh, pointing to her eyes where raccoon circles descend from where she intended her makeup to be. "One to talk, auntie."

Ash shrugs, stretches, her tight leather pants creaking

softly, matching black jacket barely covering her exposed midriff. She saunters into my space, helping herself to a handful of grapes I keep near my reading chair, settling her long-legged form down with her foot resting on her knee, more masculine but alluringly feminine. There's a charisma about Aunt Ash I know normal men can't resist. I've witnessed her take over an entire bar with a single, smoldering look around a crowded room. She's the only one in our family who doesn't share the typical dark Greek hair and skin tone, her eyes as bright blue as any I've seen.

"Kayden giving you shit again?" She tosses a grape at me, another passing her full lips. I sink into the couch across from her and shrug, trying to forget our last confrontation.

"I can handle it." I know I can. I just hate to resort to hurting him to make him back off. But if it comes down to a battle, I will do what I have to, no matter my dislike for fighting.

Aunt Ash drops her foot to the floor and leans forward. "Just kick his ass and be done with it." Her long-fingered hands fold in front of her and I wonder then as I watch her, why she's never chosen a mate of her own. Or why Sibyl hasn't forced her to take one. Then again, as my aunt winks at me, I acknowledge no one would ever be able to make Ash do anything.

Maybe I should take notes.

"Missed you at service this morning." I shouldn't tease her, maybe, but she winks at me with a drawn out grin.

"Been a little busy." She hunts around in the zippered pocket over her right breast, fishing with long fingers.

"Can I ask you a question?" I sink back into the cushions, thinking of the twins and their cryptic conversation. I've held my doubts in for so long, it feels weird to consider sharing my worries, but if anyone will hear me out and not freak on me, it's Ash.

She shrugs, sitting back herself, narrowed eyes watching me carefully. She twirls the slim cigar she liberated from her jacket and lights it with a flick of her thumb, her gold-etched lighter slightly smaller than my bulky silver box. Smoke wafts up from the glowing tip as she inhales and breathes out a stream, making three "O" shapes with careful snaps of her jaw. "Can't say I'll have answers," she says, the thick scent of flavored tobacco filling the room. "But I'll do my best."

I nod, pulling my legs up under me, knowing I'm wrinkling my robe, but not really caring at the moment. "Have you ever wondered if your interpretation of a vision was the right one?"

Ash takes another drag, staring at me through the rising smoke. She seems relaxed, but I notice her free hand twitch, fingers tightening on the arm of the chair, and I know I've done the right thing bringing this to her at last.

If Bellanca and Thanos are right, if I have a choice to make, coming soon, I need all the support I can get and Ash has always been there for me.

"Kid," she says, "if I've learned anything in this life of mine," she leans forward and taps ashes into the fireplace before creaking her leather-clad way back to reclining, "it's that there is more than black and white. There are always shades of every other color."

I nod slowly, fingers toying with the satin edging of my robe, feeling a flush of color rise to my cheeks. "So our interpretations are suspect?"

"Always." She sighs out a plume of smoke. "Thing is, there are times we can tell, you get me? Times when the visions are simple, straightforward." She taps her free fingers on the arm of the chair. "Like, seeing someone step on an icy staircase and slip and fall. Right?"

"Right. So we would find that person and stop them from going down the stairs."

She grins at me through the mist of white hovering around her. "Except," she says, "maybe that person was supposed to fall."

I bite the inside of my cheek. "That's always been the fear," I say. "The one Grandmother won't talk about."

Ash snorts smoke out her nose, tapping her cigar into the coals again. "Sibyl doesn't like thinking outside the right and wrong trap she's got everyone tied up in." My aunt's voice is harsh, though from the cigar or from anger, it's hard to tell. "I'm done playing the Oracle game, Zo. Done playing Goddess. That what you're thinking?"

I look up at her, startled. "We can do that?" It never crossed my mind. My entire life I've been lectured on duty to the family, to the gift given me by Gaia. Could I give up being an Oracle?

Ash doesn't answer for a long moment, eyes lost in the distance. When she finally does speak, it's with a wistful sadness that rouses my guilt. "I don't know," she says. "I'm doing my damnedest." Her gaze finds mine again. "You've been having doubts." Not a question. "For a while now." Again, not a question. She sighs. "I should have talked to you before this, but I wanted you to come to me."

"You knew?" If I'm that obvious, does my grandmother and her sorcerer mate also see through me?

Ash's grin is fierce. "I know you," she says. "You've been off for quite some time. But I couldn't be sure and didn't want to stir the pot if you were doing okay."

Tears rise to my eyes, burning them almost like flames, my throat tight suddenly, chest constricting. I've needed this, to have this talk with her. Yes, the conversation I had with the twins was also necessary, but this is my aunt, my mother's youngest sister and the closest thing I've had to contact with my lost parent.

Ash rises from the chair, comes to my side, tossing

her cigar in the coals before hugging me to her. I embrace her back, welcoming her steady comfort.

"Okay, kid," she says. "I may not be Leyea and Gaia knows your mother would have been a million times better at this than me. But I'm all you've got." Her own eyes are bright as she leans back and I wonder just how much of her real self Ash hides behind her powerful front. "So, tell all and not a word leaves this room."

I do so, sharing everything, including my talk with Bellanca and Thanos. She frowns at the mention of the twins, but doesn't interrupt, hawk-like focus on me while I stammer my way through two years of doubt. She prods me with one finger when I mention Piers, but her eyebrows shoot up when I tell her about Charlotte and her defense of the woman, Syd.

When I'm done, Ash crosses her arms over her chest, face unreadable.

"Any ideas why your grandmother would be lying to you?" Is that bitterness in her voice? Ash knows far more than she's saying just yet.

I fight a burst of hatred for the traitor in me even as I nod firmly. "Not entirely. But I mean to find out the truth, with or without help." I've never challenged my aunt before, but I hope she takes the hint, slightly fearful despite my determination she might try to stop me.

I'm not wrong in that regard. "Listen to me." Ash grasps my arm in one strong hand, face inches from mine, intensity so powerful I catch my breath. She's hurting me she's holding me so tight, but I don't try to pull away, lost in her blue eyes. "You don't breathe a word of this to anyone else, you hear me, Zo?"

I nod again, quickly this time, fearfully. When I speak, my voice whispers out of me. "Something's wrong here, isn't there?"

Ash lets me go, so quickly I rock back from her. She doesn't answer, just stands and turns to the door. I want to call her back, to beg her to tell me what's going on, but I hold my tongue. Just as well. She pauses with her hand on the knob and looks back at me.

"You've been in the fire too much," she says, voice gruff. "You may be the strongest Oracle born to this family since ancient times, but even you can only spend so much energy in the flames." She swallows, hesitates. "There are legends about Oracles who go too far into the fire, Zoe. Legends I'd rather you didn't prove right."

Even as I open my mouth to agree, I know I'm lying. "I'll be careful." The fire in me answers with a pleading whisper I have to bite my lip to ignore.

Ash, grim and dark-faced, seems to know I'm trying to deceive the both of us. But instead of arguing, she leaves me there, closing the door behind her.

I surge to my feet, rubbing my hands together as the skin begins to tingle. Just the mention of the flames seems to be enough to wake them, now. I need a distraction if I'm to follow my aunt's order. A quick change from my rumpled robe into jeans and a sweater and I'm slipping out of my room and down the hall to the travel hub, fingers locked around my lighter in my front pocket.

A few hours escape in the city should do the trick. Though I know the moment Piers's face passes in my mind's eye, I'm lying about my motives for this, too.

EIGHT

The flames don't want to let me go and the moment I step into them I realize my mistake. What was I thinking, after feeling them rise to greet me at the mere mention of them? I fall into the fire as I try to ride it to the surface, the pull of the flickering warmth engulfing me in need. The first instant I realize my mistake, I'm gasping for breath, panic taking over. Until I am devoured by the welcome of the fire, its love and desire for me so pure my anxious reaction dies in a burst of flame. I sink into it, embracing it, loving the feeling of it licking around my body, heating my core. It's only the faintest image of his face that pulls me out again before I'm lost to the blaze.

I stagger out of the fire into the cool air—relatively speaking—of a Los Angeles alleyway. Disorientation shakes me from head to toe, bending me in half where I gasp for air through my open mouth, nauseated but oddly aroused by the still-present pull of the fire.

Even through my loss of focus, I can feel him and know he's nearby and feel relief I've found him so soon. I look up, straightening slowly, dark hair sliding over my face as I watch him approach with slow, careful steps. My shoulders press to the concrete wall behind me, hands flat against the surface as though to hold me up, while Piers comes to a halt a few feet from me, frowning despite his small smile.

I want to run to him, to hug him, but he's still so careful around me and I worry making the first move will rush us into something I just can't handle right now.

"Zoe Helios," he says and my heart embraces his voice, the smoky warmth of it, the way it counters the coolness of his white-blonde hair and pale skin, the clear gray of his eyes. He might look like an ice prince on the outside, but a fire burns inside him. "Told you I'd see you soon."

I draw a final steadying breath and exhale deeply. "Sorry I had to go yesterday," I say. "My grandmother was calling."

"I figured," he says, frown softening, smile growing. He looks me up and down, though not in a creepy way. "Are you all right?" Did he witness my exodus? Not that he hasn't seen me travel on the flame before. The fire must have released me in his presence since it was his face that saved me from the draw of heat. Still, I'm usually much more careful.

"I'm fine." I slip my lighter into my pocket, now wondering how I'm going to get home.

If the flames are betraying me now... fear ripples through me. What if this devouring energy comes from Gaia herself? From my doubt? Is this some means she has to punish those who move against her gifts? Panic like I've never felt drives stakes of fear through me, and I stagger back against the wall again, a wash of tears escaping before I can stop them.

Piers lunges for me, catches me in his hands, holds me up as my knees crumple. Why did I never consider this possibility? I've been so arrogant, pushing the boundaries of my gifts, doubting everything I've been taught. If I'm wrong, I deserve to be consumed.

"Zoe, it's all right." He holds me against his chest, partially inside his floor-length coat. I feel the heat of his body through his thin dress shirt, the lean muscles pressing to me and I hug him on impulse, just wanting something normal to cling to. Though, he's far from normal. His darkness pools at his feet, more powerful than any sorcery I've ever felt.

"Sorry," I whisper into his chest, pulling away after a moment. While I've longed for this kind of contact, it feels weak to lean on him. No matter the visions I've had of the two of us together, the emotions I feel for him, they aren't real. At least, not yet. And maybe never if I've destroyed my true connection to my Goddess through doubt and distrust.

"Any time." He lets me go without a fight, though he remains where he is. Kayden's close proximity only a short time ago felt nothing like this. I'm not threatened by Piers, never have been. In fact, I have a powerful urge to reach up and grasp Piers around the neck, to pull his lips down to mine and enact one of the powerful foreseeings I've experienced right here and now. Instead, I run a shaking hand over my mouth and do my best to still the fear in my heart. "Want to talk about it?

"I can't." Why do I still resist him so much? We've been sharing these stolen moments for two years, and yet I haven't been able to bring myself to betray my family, to tell him anything no matter how I feel about him. He's been good enough not to ask in the past, beyond soft offers like this one. He has far more patience than I do. "I'm sorry."

Piers shakes his head, frown returning, hands held up to ward off my words. "You know I'm here for you if you need anything," he says. "No strings attached. I always have been, Zoe."

Can I believe him? My heart begs me to, but my new fear I've somehow damaged my connection to my Goddess is at war now with the resolve I felt talking with the twins and Ash.

"Why?" It's not fair of me to challenge his kindness. He's been good to me, gentle and friendly. And though I know it has to be driving him mad, not knowing who and what I really am, he's never shown me anything but sweet patience. I guess I'm just in a confrontational mood after everything I've been through the last day and a half. And I'm taking it out on the one person who has never judged or pushed me. "Why do you care?"

Piers shrugs, smiles one of his long, sultry grins, gray eyes sparkling. "You're a mystery to me," he says. "I like that, I suppose."

He likes not knowing? I catch myself laughing, just a short burst of it, feeling slightly hysterical.

"I'm no stranger to women of power," he says, leaning against the wall, looking down at me with his hands back in his pockets, the epitome of non-threatening though he has no idea the scent of him alone is distraction beyond measure. "But they are open books, for the most part. I understand them, their motivations. Why they do what they do. You, Zoe Helios, on the other hand..." He winks slowly. "You are another matter entirely. And though I wish I could convince you to trust me, I'm rather enjoying our time together, as brief as it is."

"So am I." The words are out of my mouth before I can stop them—

—*his lips are soft, but eager, his hands hot on your skin as he slips his long, lean body over yours, the fire of his spirit linking to you—*

Piers is holding my arm again as I lurch from the vision. I can't help the creeping blush heating my cheeks, though I miss his touch when he releases me. Does he guess what I saw just then? He is aware I'm an Oracle, after all, though in the dark as to how my power works. If so, he doesn't comment, simply waits for me to pull myself together.

I hug my ribs with both hands, heart pounding, before nodding to him. "Sorry," I say. "You were saying?"

If he was speaking, I missed it, but he seems willing to go on. "This might not be the best place to talk." He looks around, hands slipping back into the pockets of his longcoat. I shrug, now chilled as sometimes happens after a vision takes me. "Feel like a little sand and surf?"

A black tunnel forms beside him and I smile, body relaxing. It's our favorite thing to do, aside from walking the streets together. And we have our own personal quiet stretch of beach we found a few months ago.

Piers holds out one hand to me. "After you, Zoe."

The moment I pass through the black, the fire in me wakes, pushing back the sucking drain on my power. My own sorcery forms black flames and holds ground for the three heartbeats it takes to exit the other side. There is no pressure to remain in the fire, and the experience actually cools the need of the flame inside me. Piers stares at me as we step out onto an empty stretch of beach, the surf pounding against the sand and the cry of seabirds making me sad for some reason.

"Something's different." He shakes his head. "Are you sure you're okay?"

I'm not cold anymore. If anything, I'm too warm, the sun overhead beating down on the two of us, the simmering fire inside me adding to the heat. I shrug out of my sweater, tank-top much better suited to our location. "Better now."

Piers shakes his head, blond hair swinging around his shoulders. It's so long and looks like strands of colorless silk. I wonder how it will feel against my bare skin and have to throw sorcery at the flames to keep a vision from rising.

"I've never felt anything like your magic before," he says, taking a step away from me, looking poised and aristocratic against the backdrop of the ocean. "You have access to the fire elemental power, but it's somehow tied directly to your sorcery, not outside it." He looks at me like I'm a puzzle he'd like to decipher before grinning. "Sorry," he says. "I told you I like a mystery."

I'm half tempted to explain, the words rising to my lips. Wouldn't he love to know that unlike other magic users, our power is fed directly through our sorcery, not detached as other races. But before I can answer, a distant expression comes over his face, and I can only guess his mind is far away. After only a moment, he relaxes and smiles at me, though he looks oddly sad.

"I have to go." Piers offers one hand and I take it, though I don't expect him to bend over it and kiss the back. Just the brush of his lips on my skin is almost too much and I'm fighting the visions again. He watches with careful eyes, but doesn't ask me what's wrong, thankfully. I have no desire to tell him of the things I've seen the two of us do. At least not until I'm ready to do something about it.

I have to trust the visions know perfect timing.

"I don't want to leave you." He releases my hand despite his words. "It gets harder and harder every time, Zoe, no matter how few moments we spend together."

I shrug, lick my lips. "I know," I say, surprised when my lips keep moving. "One of these days, we need to do something about that." Did I really just proposition him so blatantly? Piers's grin tells me he's happy about it. And I am, too, Gaia forgive me. I want to know him, really know him, not just through the sexualized prequels of my visions.

"I'll meet you here," he says. "From now on. Just come to this spot and call my name with your very unusual power." Piers takes a step back, another, a tunnel of black forming behind him. "Consider me yours, Zoe Helios." And then, he's gone.

I'm tingling all over from the meeting, from fighting the visions and sink to the sand to fall into them—

—his lips burn on yours, his power engulfing you, naked skin hot against your flesh, long hair winding around your quivering body as you both moan your need into the night—

I emerge a short time later, blushing furiously, but eager to see him again, for real, in the flesh.

I might burn in a hell of my own making, but the visions I've seen tell me he, at least, is my destiny and I won't fight Gaia on that truth.

NINE

I walk the beach for a half hour, finally heading into the city. It's all the time I can risk being away from the sanctuary. Any second now, my grandmother could come looking for me and after finally agreeing to further my relationship with Piers, I can't have her interfering.

My sandals slap on the pavement as I duck into an alley and risk riding the fire. I have to try it, can't believe the flames will turn on me after all this time. Terror rises despite my attempt at reassurance, though when I reach for the flame with hesitant power, it welcomes me like it always does and carries me without incident to the entry portal at the sanctuary.

I stand there in the cool of the underground for a long moment, shaking and sending gratitude to Gaia. Surely if she wanted to punish me, if my questioning and rebellion against what I've been taught were against my Goddess, she would have taken this time to devour me completely. The fact I stand here in the quiet of the sanctuary tells me my fears were just that.

At least, that's what I'm choosing to believe for the moment.

"Zoe." I look up with a soft gasp, into angry, pale amber eyes. Liander's thin mouth frowns at me, slicked back hair from his sharp widow's peak shining with gel in the light. The portal room is a fair size, but it feels tiny with him standing there, staring at me with anger in his gaze.

"Liander." I dip a quick bow of my head. "Excuse me."

His hand snaps out, grabs my elbow as I try to slip past him. He's barely my height, dressed in a pinstriped suit and bright red tie, but he feels like a poser, someone to whom appearances are everything. I have an irrational thought his height must give him a complex when he shakes me with his hand and his power.

"You were to meet me in your grandmother's chambers last night." His fingers tighten further, grinding the bones of my elbow enough a soft cry escapes me. "Where have you been?"

How could I have forgotten? And it's not like him to fail to remind me of my transgressions loudly and with contempt.

I do my best to appear contrite. "Forgive me," I say, bowing my head again, assuming my submissive role though I hate myself for giving in so easily. "The oversight wasn't intentional."

I keep my eyes firmly on the tips of his shiny dress shoes, the seconds ticking by. I almost look up just to see his expression when he speaks.

"You've been absent minded and rebellious to orders of late," he says, turning and pulling me along with him. "Perhaps it's time we curtailed your freedom in order to remind you just how generous we've been."

My stomach clenches as I hurry along beside him, feeling a wash of his anger sizzle against me. There's nothing I can say in response. Experience has taught me I'm better off pleading my case to Sibyl.

He falls silent as well, though his temper only seems to grow in heat as he stomps his way past a few of my cousins who stare a moment before averting their eyes. What are they afraid of? That same rebellion Liander accused me of a moment ago wakes in a rush and begs to push back against him, clearly showing me his weakness. How pitiful his power compared to mine. How sad and pathetic this little tantrum of his. I remember being terrified of the sorcery he commanded when I was a little girl. But this man beside me feels more petulant and bitter than formidable.

By the time he slams open my grandmother's ornately

carved wooden door and shoves me inside her equally elaborate quarters, my anger is crackling inside me and ready to explode.

"Zoe." Sibyl rises from her chair, a heavy, throne-like seat near her fireplace. Her rooms are grand, the ceilings towering, antique furniture and a colorful Persian rug making it feel like ancient Greece. She's no exception, her coil of gray hair falling from its usual knot to hang almost to her feet, brushing against the hem of her gold-belted white robe. Though most of us have adopted more trendy apparel, my grandmother clings yet to the old country. Even her soft accent makes her feel like a true child of Delphi and always arouses awe in me.

"Grandmother." I ignore Liander's lingering anger and step to her side, kissing both of her cheeks. Her lips are as cold and dry as always, hands too as they gently grip my shoulders.

"You failed to come to us last night." There is no accusation in her face or voice, but I am well aware she is a master of guilt. This time, I accept my subtle punishment and nod.

"As I told him," I say, still not looking at her sorcerer mate, "I am truly sorry. It won't happen again."

"Of course it won't." She rewards me with a cool smile before raising an eyebrow to Liander who fumes as he pours himself a large goblet of dark wine. "It's just concerning when you fail to obey, Zoe. It worries me."

More than ever, I feel like a prisoner here. There have been times I've wriggled against her controls, but never before have I experienced this powerful surge of nervousness, like I'm in a cage I will never escape, my wings clipped.

"What did you want to see me about?" Better to change the subject and get to the point. The quicker I escape the better.

Liander's fist slams down on the table, the decanter of wine jumping under the blow. "First you will tell us where you've been."

It's hard not to show contempt, but I know doing so will only make things worse. They can't know my feelings have shifted. I focus on Sibyl who, at least, I respect. "Am I no longer allowed to come and go, Grandmother? Am I to consider myself chained to the sanctuary?"

Irritation flickers over her face. "Of course not, Zoe," she says, the smoothness leaving her voice, words taking on a bite. "But you have responsibilities, and I've been observing a rise in disobedience from you."

I am that obvious. "I like walking the distant halls," I say, telling at least enough of the truth she won't suspect there is more to it. "The center of the sanctuary is my home, but there are times the visions are too much and I need to breathe." Also true, though the extended network of maze-like halls and corridors of the underground city, long abandoned by whomever created it, no longer offer me the true escape I need. Though Sibyl would never understand that. When was the last time she even left the core?

She comes to me in a rush, embracing me with a sympathetic sigh. "My dear," she says. "You only need to tell me. I can help you adapt as the visions become stronger." She smiles, though it feels plastic to me in my present state of mind and I suddenly feel she only cares for the things I see, not for me. Ridiculous, of course. She's taken personal responsibility for me since my mother died and I'm grateful for her love and attention.

I nod, smile back though I don't feel like it. "I know, thank you."

She releases me, patting my cheek with cold finger tips. "I hope your head has been sufficiently cleared by your time above," she says, turning away from me to retake her seat. "Tonight, we do a seeking, and I want you to lead it."

I bow my head to her and don't comment. It used to be her job to lead vision seekings, but she's been placing me in that role for the last few months. I've begun to wonder if she's grooming me to take her place, though I can't see Sibyl ever relinquishing her role as our leader.

"My honor," I say. And then my traitor mind blurts a question. "Is this seeking for ourselves or clients?" Sibyl's brow furrows as I rush on. "Grandmother, I don't mean to question your leadership. But there are times I wonder at our loss of purpose."

Something hits me from behind, sending me staggering forward. I turn when I retain my balance to find Liander standing behind me, one fist raised, the same one he just struck me with between the shoulders.

"Your purpose," he snarls at me while I stare at him in shock, "is to serve the Light." He thumps his chest with that same fist. "Through me." So much rage and frustration in him, it oozes out like pus from a wound. My rebellious snap is gone in the face of his fury. He's never struck me before, and when I turn to meet my grandmother's eyes, I know I'll find no protector in her. She stares down her nose at me, cold and judging.

"Liander might be right," she says. "I may give you too much latitude, too much responsibility."

I shiver as I stand there, silent and contrite. I just want this to be over. *And then what, Zoe Helios? What will you do?* I don't have an answer to that question as my grandmother speaks again.

"You've disappointed us, Zoe," she says. "See to it that never happens again."

I bow a hasty retreat, dodging Liander and spinning to run out the door, not caring it's obvious I'm fleeing out of upset. Let them know they've hurt me, made me fear again.

They've only strengthened my resolve to find out the truth.

TEN

I slick my hands down the sides of my robe as I take my place in the center of the circle. I don't have to look up to know who watches me with waiting gazes. I know them all: aunts and cousins of varying degrees and removes. Only twelve of our number stand ready, though that large of a group makes me nervous. Most seekings require maybe five or nine. Thirteen Oracles coming together creates its own foretelling.

Liander and my grandmother are looking for something specific.

I just hope I can deliver. I've been feeling oddly since I fled Sibyl's chambers, the tingle I experienced after Piers left me stronger than ever. I rub my fingertips together to try to calm the pins and needles sensation and force slow, steady breaths. I've done this many times before, have been part of seeking circles my entire life. This I can handle. As long as the flames behave themselves.

I look up as stillness falls over the room, the doors closed on the chamber, magic sealing us inside. The first thing I see is Liander with his arms crossed, back against the wall, glaring at me. Impulse drives a frown to my forehead, but I erase it quickly, hopefully before he registers it. He's not supposed to be here. This ceremony is sacred to Oracles, the seeking of visions ours and ours alone. But he has control over all of our ways now, it appears, because my grandmother seems unperturbed at his presence.

When I turn my gaze from the leading pair, I realize Ash stands directly in front of me, hands folded in front of her. Seeing her there is almost as startling as Liander. She's kept herself apart from us for so long I barely remember hearing of her having visions anymore. And didn't she just tell me she doesn't participate on purpose, that she's pulled away from Sibyl? Ash winks slowly at me, and I smile in return. I don't know why, but I feel ten times better knowing she's here for this.

"Oracles." Liander's voice is harsh when he speaks. This time I see irritation pass across my grandmother's face, but she doesn't argue when he chooses to take her position and lead the ceremony. "Begin the seeking."

I embrace the flames inside me, their eagerness controllable, at least. Knowing so calms me further, allows me to extend my power through the sorcery tied to my fire, to link with each of the twelve Oracles around me. I've long been told seeing the future is a tricky prospect, clear visions hard to manifest. Many of the women in my family experience only brief and murky moments they need assistance deciphering. Those standing around me now are the strongest of us in reach and clarity, though I know why I stand in the center as thirteenth. I've always had a knack for finding visions, for calling up sounds and scents and crispness, even more than my grandmother. Pride feeds my power, for no matter what deceptions I endure now, the visions themselves never lie to me.

I feel Ash's firm grip, the stammering and uncontrolled touch of Rena, ten others. My magic loops around them and pulls them close, their minds my mind, their magic my magic until a great and powerful calm takes me into a river of flame and I am as close to my Goddess as I have ever come.

"Name the target." Our power turns on the puny sorcerer who dares to order us. But we are the fire and the future, questions asked and answered and we will obey the calling of our nature.

"You know the target." He practically spits the words at us. "Show her to me."

He's obsessed with her, the one he calls Dark. We turn inward, feeding the flames with our souls, and call on the future to show us what is to come.

Something is wrong, altered, out of touch. I break free of the others a moment as they fight against me. It's not until I seize them and pull them back I understand why. I no longer think of the woman Syd as the Dark One. To me, she has become the Light.

They sigh and relent, but I know I've revealed too much as I return to the center of the seeking and we are one again.

The vision surges toward us, and we welcome it, funneling it outward and above. Twelve sets of eyes look upward, twelve souls focused as I find myself again outside them, with full control. I struggle to return to the bond, but it's gone and all I can do is allow the vision to unfold and try not to panic.

Completely different, this experience. Usually I feel an immediacy with visions. This time I'm so far out of it, I can see the power holding it together, making it manifest. And feel the subtle touch of my grandmother's power around it. I almost break focus and stare at her in shock. She isn't one of the thirteen—so why then is her magic involved? I must understand this. But, for now, the vision demands my attention, no matter my distance from it.

The woman Syd appears. She seems angry, standing in a dark room that looks like a basement. The werewolf Charlotte is at her side, holding a white Persian.

"...don't care what it takes," Syd says. "We know he's

out there. We find him and see the end of this once and for all." A giant with diamond eyes bows to her. The dragon, I'm certain of it. I've seen him in full winged form, her on his back. But though he wears a more human form, I would know his energy anywhere.

Liander snarls, startling me, though I'm deep enough in the fire the vision doesn't waver.

"Will that bitch never relent?" He spins on his heel, eyes meeting mine. Does he see I'm working alone, outside the group? Does my grandmother? Neither seem to find it odd. In fact, Sibyl is frowning, eyes locked on the vision, too wrapped up in whatever her own power is doing to notice me at all. I long to check, to test her involvement, but doing so will alert her something has changed in me and I'm not sure I want her to know.

"I need to know if it's time." Liander breaks my questions into fragments, renewing my focus. I turn my face from him and focus on the vision.

It shifts to a blonde woman at a desk, a single light at her side casting shadows over her face. She rubs at the hollow of her throat where a pentagram pendant rests. She appears uneasy, unhappy, though her power surrounds her, palpable and waiting. It glows blue, witch magic, the room where she sits dark paneled and still, steeped in decades of elemental energy. A door opens and she looks up. I can't see who enters, but her face goes blank and she nods, looks down. Her fingers shake as they grip a pen, blue fire flaring over her signature. She stands, abruptly hands over a piece of paper she's signed, looking away as though unwilling to admit what she's done. I can't see who owns the waiting hand that takes the paper so eagerly. When the visitor's fingers touch it, the page flares with blue fire and black flames.

Liander is smiling now, more arrogant than ever. "How soon?"

I assess the feeling of the vision. "Within days," I say. "If not before." It's difficult at times to pinpoint exact moments, so I seek the vision for some evidence of date while he glares at me, impatient. I twist the vision sideways, look down at the desk and spot a calendar under the woman's coffee cup. She's marked off each day with a red pen, leaving her current date empty.

A swift calculation and I nod to him. "Tomorrow," I say.

He rubs his hands together, smirk ugly. "Perfect," he says. "She might be prepared, but she has no idea the pawns I have in place. Let her hunt in the dark. I'll have the law on my side."

I have no idea what he's talking about, but if he's happy about it, I should worry.

The vision begins to fade, but I'm still in control and curious. As it flickers, I tilt upward and see the recipient of the page smiling at the woman behind the desk. I know that smile, Liander's nasty expression familiar to me. But before I can wonder what need he would have for a witch, the vision flares and turns to fire, crackling and insistent.

I stare into it, forgetting Liander and my grandmother, the twelve Oracles around me. The flames beckon, pull me closer, beg for me to join them once and for all. And I lean into them, welcoming their embrace, even as fear of what is to come speeds my pounding heart.

Not now. I'm pulled back, Bellanca's magic powerful around me, though she is alone. *There's time yet.*

And she is gone, the others shaking their heads and smiling at each other as the bond dissolves in sparks, not one of them aware things nearly went terribly wrong. Or that I, somehow, remained outside them. It shouldn't have been possible. Sibyl seems to sag, massaging her temples a moment before offering her usual enigmatic smile.

Only Ash stares at me with a frank expression as the others bow to me in ceremonial thanks and leave in small, chattering groups.

ELEVEN

Ash comes to my side, takes my elbow in her hand. "Are you all right?" Her voice is low enough only I hear it.

"Fine, thank you." I offer a trembling smile. "Just tired." It's not necessary to lie to Ash, but I want to understand what's happening to me. Thank Gaia for Bellanca, though how did she know I needed her? She and her brother have gone again.

Ash releases me, but doesn't stop staring in her closed and determined way, not until Sibyl approaches with a smile, reaching out to embrace me.

"Very well done, my dear," she says, an arm around my shoulders as she faces Ash. "The finest we've raised, wouldn't you say, dear Ash?"

My aunt shrugs, grin twisted. "If you say so." She yawns, stretches inside her robe. "Thanks for the walk down memory lane. Forgot why I hated being part of this shit so much."

Sibyl glares at her, tightening her grip on me. Why is Ash purposely provoking my grandmother?

"It was your idea," she snaps at my aunt who winks at me like she finds the whole situation amusing. "I had thought perhaps you'd come to your senses and were finally rejoining the family."

"Not a chance." Ash strips off her robe and tosses it at Sibyl's feet. "Just for old time's sake. You and your little pet sorcerer might think this is the only gig in town, but I have better things to do."

"Ashtoria Marie Helios." Sibyl's voice cracks like a whip, making me jump though Ash keeps grinning. "Don't make me punish you."

"For what?" She flicks her fingers in my grandmother's face. "You don't have the balls to do anything, *Grandmother.*" I start. Wait, what? Sibyl is my grandmother. Which makes her Ash's mother. So why...? And she's stressed the moniker so much, I know it's a taunt. But why? I've only ever heard Ash address Sibyl by her first name. "Neither does that pathetic piece of crap you brought into our sanctuary."

Black power rushes toward us, and only then do I realize Liander is still here. Ash turns with a casual wave and blocks his magic before it can harm her, the slap of black scattering in a rush of broken pieces. He grunts and staggers a little while my aunt snarls at him.

"Try that again," she says. "I'll drain your ass dry."

"You may go." Sibyl's power is more formidable. Ash rocks back herself from a solid wall of fire. But her contempt isn't lessened as she shrugs, hands in the pockets of her leather jeans, sparks in her blue eyes.

"See you around," she says before sauntering out with a click of her tongue and a mock salute for Liander. I stare as my aunt slams the door behind her, turned instantly to face my grandmother before the sound of the echo is even stilled.

"You are forbidden further contact with Ash," she says, fury snapping in her gaze. "I will have her banished for this."

Banished? I want to protest. That means cutting my aunt off from the family, from the Oracles who love her. Where will she go? What will she do? I grasp for my grandmother's hand, ready to beg her to reconsider, but Liander interrupts.

"About time," he snaps. "I'm truly disappointed in how little control you have over your women." Is that anger in Sibyl's eyes? I hope so. How dare this cretin talk of our family like that? We are the Helios Oracles. He is just a sorcerer. "I'll leave you to discipline them. I have a job to do."

Sibyl starts, while my anger simmers at her lack of retaliation. Maybe they are right, but I like this new rebellious side of myself. "Already?"

He waves her off, talking over his shoulder as he goes. "Finally."

My grandmother appears troubled, and I'm going to add to her worries. I can't stand this to go on any longer and this is the first time I know I'll have her alone, without Liander listening in.

"Please tell me," I say, voice cracking as emotions run high, "we are following the true path of Gaia by helping him?"

She looks startled for the second time, as though I've slapped her, stepping away with a scowl hurriedly disguising her reaction. The rest of the family are gone, only my grandmother and I in the round chamber. "How dare you challenge my authority in this matter," she says. I can tell she's trying to be firm, but she sounds more disturbed than angry.

I shake my head, unwilling to let this go. Maybe Ash's confrontation has given me courage or the recent events have freed me to speak, but it's time at last to confront Sibyl fully. "I've spent my whole life trusting and believing in you," I say. "I've never questioned, Grandmother. But I have reason to believe the visions I've experienced aren't being interpreted truthfully."

Flames rise from her feet, sizzling out toward me. I've

made her truly angry this time, but I can't bring myself to care.

"Blasphemy!" She tries to push against me with her power, but mine is stronger than hers. Sadness pierces my heart, as I stare at her, remembering her power's interference with the visioning. What purpose could she have, unless...

"You've led us astray on purpose." I shudder and hug myself, not trying to attack her with magic, holding her off until hers drops away. "You manipulated the seeking. Didn't you?"

She doesn't answer, spluttering her way around her guilt. I know it's true, then, feel it in her power as I touch the edges of her fire with my own. "Enough, Zoe." But she's lost all authority with me. The way her eyes tighten, how her lips thin, tongue sneaking out to wet them, all of it showcases her guilt.

"Why, Grandmother?" I now realize the deepest part of the lie. The visions I believed, the foresight I've trusted my entire life... how much of it has been shaped by my grandmother? I shudder, glare at her with disbelief. "You've broken our sacred oath to channel the future truthfully and with honor. You've betrayed Gaia."

Sibyl shakes, hands clenching into fists at her side, eyes blazing with fire. She might not be striking me with power, but it's clear she wants to.

"Stupid girl," she snarls. "You have no idea what

you're talking about."

"Then why have we lost our purpose?" I throw the question at her. This isn't me, this confrontational girl, but I'm suddenly free and unwilling to let this go any longer. I must have answers from her. "Why do we only seek visions under the orders of Liander Belaisle when once we were free Oracles?" I jab a finger at her. "Why have you allowed him to control us when we are so much more powerful than he?" She doesn't answer. "And why do you influence a seeking with your own magic, if not to manipulate for some secret purpose?" I drop my hands to my sides, lost and sad. "What are you afraid of, Grandmother?"

"That's what's been wrong with you lately." Her voice is cold again, though her fire still rages inside her, around her. "You've been challenging your visions."

I hold still, jaw aching from jutting forward in defiance. So like her to turn this conversation around and try to use it against me.

"You little idiot." She wrings her hands in front of her. "I've done nothing of the sort, and would never go against the word of Gaia." My resolve cracks slightly. She sounds so insistent, so hurt by my accusation. Am I wrong? "What you felt was me protecting you, you young fool. From the outside world. Someone must do it. And I am the only one strong enough to keep you safe." No, wait. Is that true? I had no idea. But then again, I've never been outside the vision like that before.

Is she telling the truth? It makes an odd kind of logical sense...

"Zoe." She jerks me out of my spinning confusion with just the sound of my name. "Don't you know the consequences of doubting your gift?"

Hesitation and renewed nerves bubble to the surface all over again. Did I misjudge her? And by pushing against my visions, have I cause irreparable damage? What if this incident is a forerunner for something much worse? I'm flinching at shadows. Could it be my fault? I don't want to believe it, but it's so hard to counter her when I was raised to obey her. "Tell me."

She shakes her head, flames dying. "I blame myself," she says, faint despair in her voice, adding to my crumbling courage, sending shivers through the girl she trained. "I should have schooled you to believe fully and not trusted you to develop so much on your own." Guilt flickers over her face. "I thought if I raised you personally, but gave you certain latitudes, things would be different for you than they were for your mother."

My mother? My entire body stiffens. "What are you talking about?" My mother died in an accident in the city above, when I was very small. I don't even remember her.

Sibyl shudders, takes a step toward me. I hold my ground since she's not threatening. Instead, her hand rises and she touches my cheek, her fingers hot from the flames that have only recently died. "Leyea was brilliant," my grandmother says. "Powerful, almost as powerful as you." Her hand drops like dead weight to her side. "But she, too, questioned her visions. Became paranoid and rebellious. I had thought I taught you better, watched you close enough. I now see I was wrong. Like mother, like daughter."

"What are you saying?" I almost choke on the words.

"Leyea died," Sibyl says, "in the flames of her power. That's what happens to Oracles who doubt, Zoe. Who challenge the gift of Gaia."

I stare at her, open mouthed, fear surging. Dear Goddess, was I right after all? Was my guess the correct one and I've doomed myself?

"I see you still doubt," Sibyl says, taking my hand firmly in her own. "It's time I proved it to you."

I follow her as she leads me to the door, stumbling over my feet with a terrible fear growing in my heart.

TWELVE

The corridor is quiet and dark as my grandmother leads me from the ceremony chamber toward the main chapel. This stretch of hall isn't used often, so I'm not surprised we encounter no one on our hurried journey. At first she has to tug me along to keep pace, but by the time we approach the large door leading to the chapel, I'm almost ahead of Sibyl's long strides.

I love the quiet of the room as we enter, always have, feel it seep into me, calm my wildly beating heart. No matter my fear and doubt, there's nothing as pure and amazing as being this close to Gaia, where her true form lies beneath the stone casement at the altar.

My steps slow again when my grandmother releases her hold on me, sweeping forward with her white robe rippling around her and soft sandals silent on the stone floor. When she bends over the altar, her gray braid coils into a circle beneath her, moving silently sideways as the covering of Gaia's resting place slides aside.

I catch my breath, both hands pressed to my chest as she rises, surrounded by rainbow light. As she does, for the first time since I've begun seeing visions of the one known as Syd, I make a connection that sweeps the air from my lungs in a rush of shock.

Rainbow light. How can I have missed it? Syd's power...

Is Gaia's power.

Sibyl looks up, sees me gaping and must assume it's over the sight of our reposed Goddess because she smiles faintly, leaning away from the iridescent shimmer of the shielding around her. "Come, child," she says, sweeping her long fingers in a summoning gesture. "You ask for proof. Gaia has that proof."

I step toward the Goddess, hesitant and afraid, while I swallow the moment of realization I just had. If I failed to make the connection between Syd and Gaia, what else have I missed? I've been foolish to think my weak attempts to understand could possibly matter. Not when I'm dealing with power so vast as that of my Goddess.

Still, I sit next to her, looking down, though when my hand reaches out, Sibyl slaps my fingers away.

"You must never touch her," she says, stern and angry, though fear lies behind her eyes. "We are her servants, Zoe. And she is divine."

I nod, cradling my hands in my lap. It's difficult not to gaze down at her in adoration, to study the quiet stillness of my Goddess's face, the way her hair curls and coils around her cheeks. She's so pale, the light of the shielding protecting her making her seem young and old all at the same time as the rainbow flexes and flows, a living thing.

"Call the flame." Sibyl's voice barely intrudes as I seek deeper into the beauty of Gaia. "Ask her directly if what you've seen is true."

I've never believed such an honor would come to me. "Will she not be angry with me?" I would crumble into dust if my Goddess were disappointed in any way.

"Just ask."

My fingers find my lighter, pull it free from my pocket, the metal warm from being close to my skin. I barely remember opening the top, flicking the wheel, the fire coming to life. My eyes don't leave Gaia's face for a moment.

"My Goddess," I whisper to her, leaning over her. "Show me the truth and the way and I will never doubt again."

I draw a breath, feel the fire engulf me like never before—

—*Blood, there is blood everywhere, on your hands, dripping down your legs, pooling on the ground. And death, bodies scattered at your feet. Oracles you know and love, young sorcerers fallen. A sob escapes your chest as fire blazes to life, but not the loving, welcoming flames you're used to. These devour with hunger and greed, uncaring, cruel. You fall back from them, turn in time to see yourself, reflected in a mirror, your face pinched in fear as the fire engulfs you and carries you away—*

I cry out as I throw my lighter from me. My thumb burns, singed by the flame somehow. I ignore it, burying my face in my hands, sobbing my fear and heartache into them.

My death and the deaths of those I care about. I've seen the future—but can I change it? I look up with desperate hope into my grandmother's eyes. "Is it set, this vision?"

She shrugs, sighs. Is it just me, or does she seem tired, strained? Was her magic a part of that vision? Damn me, I can't seem to quell my disbelief even now, even after seeing what I've seen at Gaia's behest.

Sibyl's long arms fold over themselves as she crosses them, gaze dark. "I don't know," she says. "But it's your doubt that has led you to this future."

I stand as she moves forward, closing the stone over Gaia once again, my spiking guilt smothered as my Goddess is hidden from me. I watch her, now numb and cold inside despite the burning in my thumb, mind still as though unable to process. When the slab closes over Gaia at last, I turn away, only to feel Sibyl's arm around my shoulders.

"She called you Grandmother." I look up at her, thinking of Ash, needing the distraction.

Sibyl smiles. "There is much you have yet to learn," she says. "Much I will teach you. One day. But not today." My toe hits something hard that spins under the door. If Sibyl notices, she doesn't comment. Instead, she leads me out to the main corridor, watches from the open entry as I stop and turn back to her. "Zoe, I must know I can trust you." Her fingers slip into my hair. "You are the brightest and most powerful of us. Tell me you will abandon this rebellion and follow the ways of Gaia."

"So many secrets," I say, shoulders pulled down with the weight of recent events. "Is there any wonder I doubt?"

Sibyl's lips tighten. "Don't make me confine you to your quarters." I bob a nod, look away. "I'll check in on you later, dear." With that threatening sounding statement, she closes the doors behind her, leaving me standing alone in the corridor.

I shiver, rubbing my arms under my robe, turning with heavy feet toward the stairs and my room above. A flash of silver on the floor sends me forward, to retrieve my fallen lighter with the desperation of a child clutching for a favorite blanket. It's still warm to the touch, as though a living, breathing thing exists inside it. For a long moment I wish the fire would just consume me so I don't have to deal with what I've discovered.

But no. I've never been one to turn my back on my gift. I need to retreat, to think on what I've seen and learned. But the darkness that held me after the vision at Gaia's side begins to lift the moment I take my first step.

We know futures can be altered. Part of what we do as Oracles is to guide what is to come, to ensure everything that happens is the correct path. For good or ill, our job is to maintain the flow of time. Even if that means the deaths of many to save a few who will lead the world into safety.

Surely Gaia wouldn't allow me to see such a future without the chance to change it? But does that mean I need to stop doubting, to fall in line and obey my grandmother and her lover? I shudder at the thought of Liander's assault, know there are bruises under my robe where he struck me from behind, older ones on my elbow from this afternoon. I simply can't bring myself to trust him. And, by association, Sibyl.

My door gives way under my power, the lock turning as I close it behind me. I head immediately for the shower, immersing myself in a torrent of hot water, letting the heavy stream pummel my tense neck and shoulders. I bow my head under the flow and close my eyes, hands pressed against the stone wall as I force myself to think this through.

The pull of the flames I feel... if it is tied to my

doubt, why does it feel right? As though accepting that pull is my destiny? It's only fear keeping me from the full embrace of the fire. But according to the vision I had with Gaia, those flames will turn against me. Turn against all of us. My fault?

My fault.

No, I can't believe that. I've spent my entire life with the flames, my friends, my family. The harsh fire from the vision felt wrong, off, as though someone else controlled it. And though the blaze that beckons me seems powerful, I know it's the pure elemental force pulling me in.

My stomach clenches as I straighten, eyes snapping open. What if the vision didn't come from Gaia after all? I press both hands over my abdomen and force myself to breathe. Bile burns the back of my throat as I gasp past the shock and dive into the vision—

Blood. Bodies. Fire. And the mind of another.

My knees buckle as I sink to the stone, hugging them to me, letting the water wash over me as I sob once.

The vision wasn't from Gaia. It was from Sibyl. I was right to wonder about her magic's involvement. She manipulated me, used my fear against me. Used Gaia against me. But how? The Goddess should protect me, shouldn't she? Keep such things from happening—

I see Gaia in my mind's eye, remember the feeling I had not so long ago. And realize the last bit of truth I can handle on my own. She's asleep. Truly asleep, her consciousness far off. As much as I and the other Oracles choose to believe differently, our Goddess might be with us in body, but her mind...

My feet slip over the tiles as I scramble out of the shower, barely remembering to turn off the water. Haste pushes the towel around my body, missing most of the moisture so my bra and T-shirt cling to me, making it hard to pull on my jeans. I grasp for my lighter the moment I'm dressed, flip flops barely over my toes, heading for the door.

And I pause. I can't go out there like this. What if I run into someone and they ask me what's wrong? Can I lie convincingly enough to keep from blurting out what I've learned? Sibyl has already given me her version of an ultimatum. If she catches me in one last indiscretion, I know she'll do what she can to make me a true prisoner here.

But I have to go. I need space to think. My hand shakes as I open my fingers and look down at my lighter. I'm not supposed to travel from my rooms. The wards and protections that keep us safe from outside magic only exist in the portal gateways. If I risk it, I could be opening the sanctuary to discovery from other paranormal races, something we've managed to avoid in the centuries we've lived here under Los Angeles.

And yet, I can't bring myself to care when my mind

goes to Sibyl and the lie of a vision she planted in my head. All of a sudden, all the foreseeings I've experienced are suspect. What can I believe and what is fake? Before I can stop myself, allow guilt or fear to stay my hand, I flip open my lighter and strike the wheel. My thumb stings from the earlier burn, but the flame is strong, dancing happily over the wick and I reach for it with a surge of relief.

This can't be wrong, these flames that embrace me, the blaze of heat that welcomes and warms me so much. I turn in the embrace of the fire, opening my arms to it, ready to let it take me forever, if that is what it wants.

The flames seem to chuckle, giggle like little children, before releasing me gently onto a sandy beach. I stare around me in the darkness, lighter tight in my hand, and wonder why I'm here. I didn't ask for the fire to carry me to the place I might find Piers. I've never traveled this way without a destination in mind.

Does the fire have a mind of its own?

So much I don't know. I reach for Piers, sending his name out into the ether through the power of my sorcery and the flames of my foresight. As I stand there, waiting for an answer, I wonder what I'm going to tell him. How much I plan to share. But the moment he steps out of a black tunnel, gray eyes smiling at me, I know I will give him all the secrets of my people.

I don't need a vision to tell me that.

He comes to me, gently touches my cheek with cool fingers, smiling in a sultry and welcoming way that reminds me of the flames. How they can be childlike at times, parental even, can shift to the embrace of a lover. I see his worry for me, his playfulness and the desire in his heart there in his gaze, wide-open to me. Trusting.

"Zoe," he says. "I've missed you." His lips find mine and, in that moment, I'm breathless and lost in him, forgetting everything that came before. All the hurts and fears and worries dissolve under the pressure of his mouth, the way his hands carefully but firmly hold my body against him. This heat is far different from the flames I know so well. Perhaps diving into this particular fire would be a good thing after all.

When we part, I sigh into his still-open mouth, a quirk of humor finding its way into my heart. "So forward," I say, panting a little.

"I guess I'm just tired of waiting for you to decide you're in love with me." His wink makes my knees weak, though from the teasing tone in his voice and the way his eyes sparkle, I know he's teasing me.

Or is he?

I only wish this moment could last forever. But as Piers pulls me gently toward him for another kiss, memory surges and I gasp in shock. "I can't." I push him away, more roughly than I meant to. "I'm sorry."

Piers doesn't grow angry, only concerned, though he

drops his hands to his sides and keeps his distance while I clutch at my aching stomach, tight with renewed tension.

"Zoe," he says. "I have no idea what you're going through. Partly because you won't tell me." He sighs, humor gone. "I'm not sure how to convince you I'm not a threat. That you can trust me. But from what little you have told me over the last two years, I'm guessing trust isn't something you're used to handing out to people outside your family."

I nod, biting my lower lip, so near to blurting everything to him I'm sure I'll just burst instead. Fortunately, he goes on and saves me from blubbering all over him.

"I come from a secretive family, too," he says, hands rising and falling as though he wants to hold me again but doesn't know if his offer would be rejected. "Which means, I know this can't be easy. But I'm not asking you to believe in me." He closes the distance again at last, one hand sliding into my hair, tilting my head back. "I'm asking you to believe in yourself. In what you feel when you're around me. Because I trust you, Zoe. With my life."

His head bends and his lips part and I throw every fear I've ever had away and kiss him back for the second time. A sharp moment of memory mixed with a vision tightens a noose around me and I tremble with it. I've seen this moment, felt his lips on mine, the press of his body in this exact instance. I had no idea it would happen now, but it feels the same. He feels like heaven—

—*she stirs, the rainbow shield shimmering as it flickers out and her eyes open, someone standing over my Goddess's sleeping form*—

I gasp, pull back from Piers.. When I stare up at him, I know he sees my terror, but he doesn't try to hold me back.

"I have to go." The woman with Gaia. I don't know her, have never seen her before. She isn't an Oracle, or a sorcerer. And that means someone has penetrated the sanctuary. My fault? I flinch at the thought. I've been traveling outside the protections, leaving us open to discovery. But I can't stay here and risk leaving Gaia to the mercies of a total stranger.

I reach for my lighter, find it still in my hand. Stare at it a moment, my mind trying to recognize the shiny metal pressed to my palm. When I look up again, Piers nods, though his worry is back. "I'm sorry. I shouldn't have come." I needed him, I still do, but this has to take precedence. And yet, I long to remain, to throw my arms around him again, to explore what we could be together. And to trust him as I've trusted no one in my life.

"Can I help?" His hands stretch out to me, palms up, fingers spread.

I hesitate, wish things could be different. That I'd shared far more than I had in the past. That kiss, the moment of our vision, has woken something in me, memory compounded by foresight. For the first time, I trust Piers completely. But I can't take him with me, not now. I shake my head, step back another pace, flick open my lighter and ignite the flame.

"Thank you." My gratitude slips from my lips that still taste like him. "For trusting me. I promise, the next time I see you, I'll tell you everything."

He smiles at me, a sad expression. "I look forward to it. Be safe, Zoe."

I leave him there, brow creased in concern, and race into the flame, for home, for the sanctuary.

For Gaia. I have to be there, can't miss the moment I've foreseen.

I must protect her at all costs.

THIRTEEN

I step out into my room again, panting in my haste, no time to wonder why the fire brought me here and not directly to the chapel. Perhaps I should fear I've twice now ridden the flame without a destination in mind, but my connection to the blaze inside me is stronger than ever and in it I now fully trust.

But I will trust in no other, at least of my kind, not until I speak to Gaia myself.

It's late, late enough I have the halls of the sanctuary to myself as I rush down the stairs and to the main corridor. I pause at the bottom, mind finally shifting into caution mode, holding me back from simply dashing the distance to the chapel doors and throwing them wide.

The vision felt immediate. But that could mean now, tomorrow, any time in the next twenty-four hours. I must be careful. Surely Gaia's waking will mean a shift in Liander and my grandmother, perhaps for good and perhaps for ill. Either way, I want to reach Gaia myself, before anyone else knows she's awake, so I can ask her directly.

Imagine the arrogance, thinking my Goddess would even care to answer my questions. But if I'm to understand fully this power I carry, if I'm to use my foresight for the good of all, I must hear from her directly what it is I'm meant to do.

My grandmother's interpretations, fed by Liander's needs, are suspect.

I slip into the dining hall, heading for the kitchens. Two servant girls look up, surprised, when I enter, but I grab an apple from a bowl on the wide table near the door and salute them with it. Both smile and go back to the giant mound of bread dough they are kneading. The kitchen's low ceiling catches the scent and makes my stomach growl, but I hurry on, through the giant space, past the bank of stainless steel ovens hot and ready to bake tomorrow morning's bread, and out the servant's door.

The sanctuary is a warren of corridors and linked passages. As a child I spent endless hours wandering them, a practice mostly halted when Liander appeared and moved in full time, and my duties as an Oracle became paramount. While it's true these tunnels and passages were my old haunts, it's been years since I truly explored them, despite what I've led Sibyl to believe. I struggle to remember the way, though the girl I was has no trouble when I finally relax and let her lead. Within a few minutes, I'm easing open a small wooden door behind a heavy tapestry and peeking into the main chapel.

The altar is silent and dark, the stone cover over Gaia's resting place closed. I leave the door ajar and sneak in anyway, flip flops making soft sounds as I pad my way to the altar. I stand over the place where Gaia rests and look down at it, feeling for her. There are protections over the casing, thick and black, tied to sorcery. I feel my grandmother's power in them, but even more so, I feel Liander's. And his isn't autonomous. How odd. Sibyl's magic is separate, encapsulated. But a thread ties Liander to the shields and I feel a pulse of power as I start to pull away.

He's feeding the shielding still? Is that what's weakening him? A moment of guilt I've somehow misunderstood and misjudged him tweaks my conscience. Could it be he's been protecting her with his sorcery all along, and it's been draining him?

But no, I see my error almost immediately as another small pulse of magic exits the shields and runs down the thread. Away from Gaia. And my hands clench at my sides, my jaw aching as my teeth grind together and flames flare in my heart.

He's feeding off her.

I sink to my knees, hands falling to the surface of the stone. How did I miss this? I am an Oracle, a foreseer, supposedly the most powerful in many generations. His deception should have appeared to me. Shouldn't it? If not, what is the point of seeing the future if I can't protect the Goddess who grants me my power?

I should sever the connection. It's my first impulse. Tears splash from my eyes to the granite, shimmering a moment before the rock absorbs them. Does my grandmother know?

Dear Gaia. She must know.

I gasp for breath, rocking back on my heels, fear holding me back. If I sever the connection, if I even attempt it, Liander will know. I have to tell the others, show them first, make them pay attention. Even if that means turning the family against my grandmother.

Aunt Ash. Her face flashes in my mind as I paw the tears from my face. I have to find her. She'll stand with me, I know it.

Just as I rise to run off, heart pounding, chest aching, I feel something stir under the stone. The touch freezes me in place. It's there, under the oozing black of Liander, under the rainbow shielding. I let my flames slip beneath.

And touch her as she sighs. She grips my magic with hers. Massive, ancient, and yet reduced to a breath of power, a faint echo of what once was. She holds me only for an instant, but long enough to prove my vision right. She's waking. I have no time to lose.

I almost forget to return the way I came. I'm shaking and I'm certain white-faced, a state that would rouse suspicion and questions should I encounter any of my fellow Oracles in the main corridor. I have enough time to catch my breath and rub circulation back into my cheeks as I retreat, though my heart is broken at my revelations. Liander, devouring our Goddess. Once powerful, now reduced. By his feeding? But no, it would take far more than the thin bit of magic he's stealing from her to bring her so low.

I stagger past the edge of the tapestry and head for the kitchen, my power reaching out for Ash even as I jog as best I can in flip flops. I can't feel my aunt anywhere in the sanctuary and curse softly as I stumble over the lintel and into the kitchen. This time I don't bother with subterfuge, ignoring the worried looks from the girls still making bread like the world I've known my whole life isn't shattering around me.

My feet skid as I turn out into the dining hall, brushing noisily past a few chairs before catching my balance, mind still desperately hunting my rebellious aunt. By the time I slide to a halt in the main corridor, I know she's not here and I'm on my own.

I make it five steps, heading for my grandmother's room, confrontation on my mind, when a hand reaches out of the dark and jerks me though a partially open door. I meep a cry of surprise before a second hand clamps over my mouth and pulls me backward. I hear footsteps now, many of them, and low voices talking. The stench hovering around me triggers a memory response just as Rupe turns me around and stuffs me into a closet, slipping silently in behind me. He pulls the door closed almost completely, peeking out through the slit, the tiny shaft of vertical light casting a weird glow on his grinning face, making his eye look transparent.

"Shhh," he hisses, before smothering a giggle behind his hands as his sorcery envelops me in a smothering blanket. My flames whisper to a hush, though images become sharp edged and the barest sounds are amplified. Whatever Rupe has done, he means to hide us while giving us the opportunity to see and hear everything.

I almost balk at being controlled this way. But the sound of the door at the other end of the room opening, and the crisp, angry tone of Liander's voice, tells me I need to stay where I am.

"...certain, master?" That sounds like Kayden.

"Silence, you young fool." Liander is furious, it vibrates in his words, though he keeps his voice down. "I know what I felt." I lean around Rupe, ducking under him to peek out myself. We're in the main study, I realize, the walls lined with the recorded foresights of my people. How ironic. "Go to the altar and make sure she's still contained."

I catch a sliver of a glimpse of Kayden saluting, a pair of young sorcerers leaving my view, clearly following orders. Another of his men joins him as Liander glares at the floor.

"Tell me what you need, my master." Liander's second in command, Paster, can't be more than twenty-five and carries the weight of his duties like a much older man. He even has early gray at the temples of his dark hair, a bald patch growing at the crown, visible when he bows his head.

Liander waves him off, brows drawn together, teeth nibbling at the edge of his mustache. "I'm done waiting for the perfect opportunity." His gloves slap against his leg, velvet robe swinging around his shoulders as he turns to face Paster. "It's time to move on her, to take full control."

Paster visibly swallows. "You've done wonders convincing her," he says, stuttering over his words. "But, considering what we're trying to accomplish, I fear we'll lose her if we push too hard."

"I couldn't care less for the state of her mind or her conscience." Liander's anger burns with its own kind of fire. "I've put too much faith in Sibyl and her damned Oracles, only to fail time and again." It has to be painful for him to admit. "And now the old woman is losing control, we're out of time." Again he slaps his gloves against his leg, this time pacing out of my view. I keep my eyes locked on Paster while my ears follow the tread of Liander's feet over the stone floor. "I need the power the witch controls to regain ground. And this is the only way to do it."

Paster nods quickly, bows. "Of course, master," he says. "We'll tighten the knot at once."

Liander reappears in my view, snarling. "Even with the benefit of foresight," his words rumble from him with a harsh edge like the cut of a knife, "knowing exactly what was coming, that Hayle bitch still manages to find a way around fate." Black ropes coil up from the floor to caress his legs and I flinch knowing some of the power soothing him comes from Gaia. "How does she do it?"

Paster doesn't answer, though my mind burns with fury. This is the final proof I need. He has been manipulating us, using us against Syd and her friends. Against Piers. I hug myself as I watch, though my eyes narrow at the thought of finding a way to defeat Liander and rescue my family from him.

Liander spins in a circle, glaring at the wall not far from where I watch, Rupe hovering over me. "A lot of good owning the Oracles did me." I almost smile at his bitterness, wishing he could see my contempt. Should I burst out, confront him here and now? No, I need the power of my sisters behind me.

He'll pay soon enough for trying to control the future.

"Your success is inevitable, master," Paster says, voice vibrating with belief.

Liander shrugs his shoulders, as though to settle his cloak about him more closely, face composed. "No matter the fools I've had to deal with," he says, "the simple minds of women I've had to endure, the touch of their leader I've borne despite my disgust." If only Sibyl could hear him now. "They still don't understand the true power they possess." He sighs, gusty and frustrated. "No matter. Their magic has served to bolster mine, and I will seize the last of it when the time comes." He gestures to Paster who nods with eagerness while my heart constricts. "Are our people in position?"

Paster's grin is cruel and eager. "The Steam Union will answer your call when you're ready to make your move."

Steam Union. I've heard that term before. Didn't Piers ask me if I was Steam Union once? But who are they?

"Tomorrow night." Liander strides past Paster toward the door, leaving my view again. "Don't fail me."

The door closes, Paster's anxiety showing on his face before he turns and straightens his shoulders. "You heard our master," he says to sorcerers I can't see. "The three of you go to Harvard and lean on her as hard as you dare. But make sure she's ours before dawn."

And then they are all moving, black robes sliding past

the crack I see through and gone again, out the door.

I squeak a soft protest as Rupe casually pushes open the closet and steps out into the now empty room. My knees ache from crouching, and I take a moment to stretch them out while my mind whirls. I almost feel burned out, as though I've encountered too much, learned more than my poor brain can handle in a very short time.

When I look up, I find Rupe grinning at me, one side of his face morphing from deformed wolf muzzle and back again, his half-bald pointed ear the last thing to retreat.

"Almost time now," he sing-songs the words, dancing in a circle. "Syd's going to get what's coming to her."

Before I can stop him, ask him questions I'm sure he won't answer, Rupe dashes from the room and disappears, leaving me there to shake and wonder.

FOURTEEN

My room embraces me like an old, familiar friend, though I don't plan to stay here long. I have no idea who Liander is trying to harm or control, though if she's at Harvard, it can't be one of my people. Whoever it is, I have a feeling Piers needs to know. I could wait, try to have a vision, but the world outside the sanctuary is a mystery to me in many ways. If I can tell Piers what I know, maybe he can help me figure out what Liander is really up to.

That Hayle bitch. At least I know who she is. And that she's a friend of Piers and Charlotte. And though I owe her no allegiance, I now understand she's not the evil Dark One I've always thought. In fact, if she's Liander's enemy, I'll gladly call her friend. If I can give her a fighting chance, I'll do it.

The flames hug me close, but don't hamper my journey, leaving me alone on the beach. Is it my imagination or do they feel sad, as worried as I am? Surely not. The fire is elemental, pure and untouched by emotion outside the capricious feelings of pure energy. And yet, I'm certain they whisper their fears to me as the flames release me.

I call for Piers, not caring who hears me, standing there in the late evening, waiting for an answer that never comes. Something huge looms, perhaps is already begun. It's possible he's wrapped up in it. This Steam Union he mentioned, that he asked me about. Are they friends or foes? From the sounds of things, they are the enemy, though when Piers first asked me if I was one of them, there was hope in his voice.

I'm so confused, things are moving too quickly for me to process and I have so few answers to a million questions about a magical world I know nothing about. The visions I've trusted my entire life have been corrupted by my grandmother, by the beliefs of Liander Belaisle. If I'm to truly understand, I must examine them with this new, open honesty in my heart, my doubt now certainty something is terribly wrong.

My attempts to reach the fire, to see the truth, amount to nothing. No visions come to me, no fresh awakenings and awarenesses. It's possible either the control Liander has over Gaia is keeping her from showing me anything new, or there is simply nothing new to see.

I refuse to consider the third option. That I can no longer call up the future thanks to my actions. I know better. Gaia would not abandon me now.

Time passes slowly, though I wait only another ten minutes or so, calling out at intervals. No reply. I can't wait here forever. Instead, I embed fire into a stone and leave it where Piers will see and feel it, the glow of the rock softened by a hint of my sorcery. He'll know I was here, at least, looking for him. For now, I have another job to do.

I step out of the fire into the portal room, surprised not to find myself in my quarters. When I raise my eyes and meet Kayden's eyes, I stare in shock as he approaches.

"You've been traveling outside the protections." He doesn't even try to hide the pleasure he takes in catching me. "You're lucky I felt you coming and diverted you to safety."

The bastard. I want to lash out and claw him, pound him with flames and darkness, but he's faster. He pins me with his arms, backing me into the wall, his sorcery smothering me before I can push him back. My fire fights valiantly against him, but he's already surrounded me and every attack I try is absorbed, making him stronger and draining me.

"Let me go." I pant against his chest, keeping my head down. A tendril of black tucks under my chin and forced my face upward. His lips hover over mine, a sheen of sweat on his skin, cheeks red, eyes blazing with the need to hurt.

"You were promised to me." He kisses me roughly, fighting to hold me in place while I thrash in his arms, a tang of blood against my teeth as he cuts me with the pressure of his mouth. He pulls back, licking at his lips, grinning at my distress. "And I'll have you. With or without your consent." He chuckles, deep and angry. "Don't worry. You'll learn to like it if I have to beat it into you."

His lips descend again. I can't let him touch me, not like this, not ever. A massive eruption cracks at the base of my power and fire and fury rush out and upward. The fire bursts free in a raging ball of flame. He staggers back with a cry, batting at the smoldering blaze licking up his cloak, sorcery slamming against me. But the fire in me won't be denied. I feel it swell to fill me, spilling outside me, flooding the room, devouring everything. This is the power I feared, the fire I saw in my vision with Gaia. But it's mine to control and it will not be stopped until it has what it's come for.

The whole world swirls in oranges and reds and sparks of blue, my breath smoke and flame, my hands red-hot. Kayden scrambles away, eyes huge and afraid, but I don't care. Compassion is nothing in the face of my heated rage.

Something hits me hard, and I turn with cold fury to see Aunt Ash, a curtain rod in her hand, the tapestry at the back of the room on the floor, smoking. She stares at me with real fear, but her hands are steady on the rod she's struck me with.

There is no pain. I barely felt the attack. But the distraction is enough to cool the fire, to force its retreat, until my vision clears and I wobble with the release.

Kayden runs away before I can say anything or stop him from leaving, though I'm happy he's gone. Ash swears, the sound of metal hitting stone echoing in the room as she runs for me, the rod dropped and forgotten. She catches me the moment before I keel over, keeping me upright and moving me forward when I'm sure my feet won't move.

"You stupid girl," she hisses at me. "What have you done?"

I'm almost myself again by the time Ash unseals the locks on my door and pushes me inside. I want to ask her how she managed to get past my personal protections when she slams the door and spins on me, temper making her whole body shake.

"What were you thinking?" She runs both hands through her blonde hair, stomping two steps forward in her heavy black boots before grasping my arms and shaking me.

My teeth rattle together before I can pull away. "He attacked me."

She shakes her head, hair a lion's tawny mane, almost on fire itself as it flows around her like a living thing. "Zoe." Her voice cracks as she pulls herself together, hands fisted at her sides, feet braced wide apart as she breathes deeply and stares at me.

"Something is happening." I sink to the arm of the sofa, hugging myself. "Liander and his people are planning..."

"What?" She waits for my answer with clear impatience.

"I don't know!" I toss my hands in the air, stand and turn toward the fireplace. "But I do know he's been using us, Ash. All of us." I spin back to her. "Taking our power. Manipulating our visions. And stealing magic from Gaia." My throat tightens as I speak that truth out loud. "He's been draining our Goddess."

Ash doesn't react the way I expect. She grows calmer with each word I speak and I wonder whose side she's really on. "Listen to me." She exhales heavily before fixing me with her blue eyes. "I told you to keep your mouth shut. Have you?"

I nod. "I don't know who to trust." I jut my chin at her, so she knows she's included on that list.

Ash snorts a laugh, relaxes slightly. "Don't be a jerk,"

she says. And shudders, like an anxious dog shedding water. "Stay here." She reaches into her pocket, retrieves her lighter. "Kayden's little temper tantrum shouldn't cause you trouble. He knows if he says anything, he'll have to admit he attacked you."

I doubt that would stop him. "Where are you going?" Her gaze flattens, tells me nothing. "Just stay," she barks. "And for Gaia's sake, don't do anything stupid. I'll be right back."

She flicks her lighter, jumping into the flame before I can stop her. Leaving me to pace my room, startled by every tiny sound, certain it will be Liander at the door, come to enslave me. But the seconds and then minutes tick by and I'm left to think.

Never a good thing. Not with so much left to be worked out. I have to talk to Piers, but my family has to come first, don't they? Once they know what Liander and my grandmother have been up to... I halt my pacing, cold fear running fingers over my flesh. What if they all know? What if I'm the only dupe? I shake my head and resume tracking across the carpet from the door to the fireplace. No, that's foolish thinking. There might be a few—like Ash, obviously—who know the truth, but I can't believe my entire family are involved.

Doubt whispers dark thoughts. What if my grandmother knows exactly what she's doing and I'm being led astray by the fire trying to consume me? Maybe

Liander is trying to prevent a disaster from happening and is just a jackass on the outside?

But no, that moment of weakness dies when I remember the touch of Liander's magic siphoning power from my Goddess. Is she trapped, then, not sleeping after all? I believed she was with us by choice, but she's never spoken or opened her eyes or addressed us directly. We chose to accept Liander's explanation her mind is busy elsewhere, body trusted to our care.

Life here in the sanctuary was so different when I was a child. I remember being happy but focused, thrilled with my ability while some of the other girls were terrified. I'd always felt Gaia powerfully inside me, even more when Liander brought her to us—confirmation to me she was who he claimed. But the joy of my childhood died when he arrived, and since then I can only recall duty laced with anxiety and need.

If only we'd been permitted to commune directly with our Goddess. Perhaps things would have turned out differently. But the shielding keeping her from us has only allowed us to feel her power—not her soul.

At least, for me, until now.

My entire being aches for Gaia suddenly, the need to run from my room, to take the flame to her and free her from Liander is almost my undoing. I instead force myself to collapse into the soft cushions of the couch and deep breath myself under control.

I will wait for Ash. And together we will free our Goddess and our people. But to do that, I need answers, the kind of answers I might be able to gain from visions now that my mind is clear and open. But I must know if my grandmother is a full part of this manipulation, if she is complicit with Liander's plans or just acting out of a false sense of loyalty to him. And in order to find out, I must examine my most recent foresight, the one I experienced at Gaia's side.

I can only hope I'm wrong, that this investigation will prove Sibyl has nothing to do with the sorcerers and their plotting. It's possible, though not likely. Still, I have to know.

The lighter in my hand is heavy, like a stone, though I welcome the flames when I summon the spark from the wheel and descend with intent—

—*Blood. Bodies. Fire. But wait, beneath that vision, deeper, the touch of one you know. Influencing you, throwing darkness into your path. Manipulating the outcome of the vision, to the worst possible result—*

Sibyl's power ripples in subtle touches through the vision. And I'm proved right even as the flames pull me deeper. And at last, I know this isn't wrong, that challenging the lies I've been presented with is the only way I can uncover the truth and fully embrace my foresight.

I give in to the flames, let them burn away the false

leads and misrepresentations of my visions. I see so clearly now, as I dive through the future—

—*You sigh in sadness at the deception, the way you've been controlled and told for so long the one you're meant to trust is your enemy. She smiles at you through the rippling flames, her power as pure as Gaia's, her purpose your purpose. You must help her, the one named Syd, warn her of what is to come. You spiral forward, in darkness, flying on fire over the world, landing in a back yard where she waits, looking surprised, but not afraid. And you feel the heat of the flames engulf you as you rise again and burn up in a blazing flare—*

I cry out against this death I see, the first true vision I've had in years, but the fire holds me tight and pulls me downward into its burning depths.

FIFTEEN

Someone slaps me, so hard I jerk upright, mind still on fire, breath panting smoke into the air. Ash hovers beside me, Rena clinging to my hand, though she looks terrified and ready to run.

I cough out another puff of smoke before gagging on the taste. Ash thumps me between the shoulder blades while I bend in half over my knees, finding myself lying on the floor.

Rena blubbers a moment, trying to speak, but indecipherable as her voice rises to a wail. Ash glares at her, snapping her fingers in my cousin's face, breaking her fearful spiral.

"Enough!" Rena whimpers, lower lip catching between her teeth, brown eyes huge as they lock on Ash. "Hush, you." My aunt returns her attention to me, examining me carefully with her sharp blue gaze. "How do you feel?" She grips my chin in hand, turning my face from side to side while I catch my breath, looking back and forth between my eyes with intensity I've never seen in her before. "Can you talk?"

I nod, swallow bitterness that can only be ashes, and pull free of her hand. "I'm okay." My words are dulled by the soreness in my throat. I feel like I've swallowed live coals, but lived to tell about it. Fire burns in my belly, begging to be free.

"No," Ash snaps. "You're not."

"Zo-eee." Rena drags out my name in her quivering voice, high pitched from her fright. "You were *burn*-ing."

I squeeze her hand to comfort her and try to stand. Ash helps me while Rena steps aside, still weeping, hands wringing in front of her. I look down at myself, at the skim of gray on my skin, the pattern of burn on the carpet, and shudder off a fall of flakes that float gently to the floor.

Ash snaps her fingers at Rena again. "Make yourself useful. Water."

Rena just stares at her, still crying with growing volume. I push Ash aside and go for the pitcher myself, pouring a shaking glass and downing it in three gulps. My throat feels better, but my insides are sizzling still and I wonder if the sensation of burning from the core out will ever go away.

So close. I turn with a fresh glass, sipping this time, the tremor in my hand stilling enough I don't spill it all over myself. Ash glares like I broke some rule she set while Rena quivers and weeps.

"What the hell were you doing?" Ash's voice shakes, her own stress finally showing.

"I had to know." I lower the glass as her eyes flicker sideways to Rena. But I don't care who knows now. The truth will be coming out, just as soon as I pull myself into order and can confront my grandmother. "I saw the truth, Ash. All of it."

She hisses at me, but not before Rena stills and looks back and forth between us, both hands rising to wipe tears from her face. I catch the calculated look in my cousin's eyes, know she's over her worry for me as quickly as she's caught scent of a juicy bit of story she can tell.

"What truth?" She meets my eyes, her curiosity a living thing in her gaze. How have I missed how petty and small Rena is? Are they all like her? If so, no matter what I say or bring to them, my family is not strong enough to do anything about it.

"Mind your own business." Ash steps between me and Rena, cutting off my view of her just as anger flashes over my cousin's face. My aunt's temper is sharper, though.

Silence. Her voice ricochets in my head. *If you know*

what's good for you.

I know she's the wrong person to rebel against, that Ash may be the only one on my side, but I'm tired of carrying this alone. She must see the defiance in me, because she spins and grabs Rena by the arm, forcefully propelling the girl toward my door. I open my mouth to protest, try to take a step, feel my knees buckle and realize I just don't have the energy to fight right now.

Rena squeals in frustration as Ash pushes her through the open door. I look away as my aunt slams it in the younger Oracle's face. The chair is close, so I let myself fall into it, taking another drink of water.

Ash joins me, crouching in front of me, and I'm surprised to see her anger is gone. She sighs, takes my free hand in hers and squeezes it, fear for me all over her beautiful face.

"Zo," she whispers. "Tell me what you saw."

I do, all of it, and follow up with the way it felt to fall into the fire. She looks away, sniffs softly, one hand rising to swipe over her cheek. Is my aunt crying? The strongest woman I've ever met, tough as nails, really shedding tears? For me, or for our people?

When Ash turns back, her face is bleak and pale. "I was worried this might happen," she says. "You're too damned smart for your own good." Her smile is weak, but present. She stands, pulling me up beside her. "We don't have much time. Rena will no doubt run off to her mother or to Sibyl and blab about your event." I want to ask Ash what happened, but the shape of my body in soot on the floor tells me more than enough.

"Would I have burned up?" I stare at the outline of my body.

Ash doesn't answer that question. "They might not like it," she says, "but you need to know everything now. Our timetable has been moved up and there's nothing they can do about it."

I meet her eyes, frowning as I watch her open her lighter and flick the wheel. "Wait, what? Who?"

Ash's hand tightens on mine. "You'll see soon enough," she says. And pulls me into the fire after her.

SIXTEEN

We step out of the flames together, into a cool night breeze. I hear the pounding of the surf nearby, but it's too dark to see the ocean. A small, two-story cottage sits before us, surrounded by an overgrown but welcoming garden, an old wooden swing-set creaking softly on the right. The light is on, enough to cast shadows back from the climbing bushes and long grass that border the small lawn, lighting the path of beach rocks leading to the back door.

I hold my place as Ash turns to me, her brow tight, but her hand on my arm gentle and supportive.

"This probably won't be pretty," she says, just as the door opens and a handful of people spill out into the yard to stare. I look over her shoulder at the mix of emotion crossing their faces and understand her meaning. One of the men looks so angry I worry he might come after us. He's big, too, burly through the shoulders, a full beard making him appear bear-like and dangerous.

I'm not afraid, despite his animosity. I can take care of myself. The flames surface, waiting for me to summon them as I step past Ash and face the six men and women now watching me. At least some of them just seem anxious, whispering to each other while my aunt waves with one of her smug grins.

"What the hell were you thinking?" The big man's rumbling voice silences the mutters passed among the others. I feel Ash's demeanor shift from arrogant to irritated and reach out to hold her back as she snarls back at him.

"It's time, Baird." She snaps his name with familiar temper. "Zoe needed to be read in long ago."

I have no idea what she's talking about, but I have a feeling these people, this situation, are going to change everything about my life. And, privately, I feel a surge of relief, though I don't yet have any answers. But the feeling I'm trapped in the sanctuary—a feeling I've been enduring for the past two years, if not longer—is stripped away. Because I can sense the sorcery in these people and, in a few of the women, the fire. Oracles, escaped from the control of Liander and Sibyl.

What other explanation is there?

The big man stomps two steps forward, though he

flinches from my gaze when his brown eyes meet mine. Is that fear under his bluster, then? Why is he afraid of me?

"You've ruined everything." He chops through the air with one big hand, fingers tightening into a fist at the end of the movement. I breathe in the scent of lavender and wild roses and feel an even deeper calm take hold of me, the barest hint of salt from the ocean reminding me of my need to talk to Piers.

"Oh, hush, Baird." I didn't notice her before, though perhaps she's only just emerged from the doorway. She's shadowed by the light behind her, caught in the dark space on the step between the glow coming from inside and the illumination over the porch. Still, a shiver runs through me at the sight of her and I hesitate, a frown pulling at my brows. The feeling I know this woman is almost impossible to deny. She steps down into the grass, the barest touch of light over her cheek before both sources are behind her, cloaking her once again in shadow. "I agree with Ash. Zoe belongs here, with us. And it's time we admitted we need her."

Baird backs down, but from his deeply creased scowl I know he doesn't agree. I keep my attention focused on the woman approaching us, find myself smiling as her features finally come into clarity only a step or two from Ash and me. My chest tightens, air compressing in my lungs as she turns and hugs my aunt, kissing both of her cheeks. She's smaller than Ash by at least six inches, closer to my height, with my dark, curly hair, my brown eyes.

"You're an Oracle. A Helios." But she's more than that, I know the truth even as I choke out the words and she turns to smile at me with gentle eyes.

"Zoe." Her voice cracks. "I'm so happy you're here." It can't be her. She's dead. I was told she died, when I was very small. But it is, I know the sound of her voice though it's been years since I heard it and as I stumble forward and hug my mother, I sob uncontrollably and release the pain I've held deep inside for so long.

It's easy to ignore the renewed whispering while my mother's arms hold me tight and her lips touch my temple. If I had my way, I would never let her go. But, after what seems like only a moment, she gently pushes me back and I let her, misery and hope and love all hunching my shoulders forward as I savor the scent of roses clinging to me. From her.

She blinks away tears, touching my cheek with her fingertips, lower lip trembling. "My darling Zoe." Mother coughs softly before composing her face to calm. "I've missed you, my dear."

I clear my own throat, rubbing gooseflesh from my arms, feeling suddenly awkward and exposed. Ash joins my mother, stepping back from me, as though forming a line I can't cross. I look back and forth between them, heart aching while a sizzle of anger wakes and won't be denied.

"They told me you were dead." I believed them, even Ash. Who knew better. The sizzle turns to a slow burn I'm not sure I care to control. Relief spins into fury quickly, so quickly. "You lied to me." My own mother. Has anyone I loved ever told me the truth? "You're as bad as Sibyl."

She flinches from those words, turning her face from me while Ash sighs.

"It's not Leyea's fault, Zo." My aunt shoves her hands into the front pockets of her leather jeans. "We all decided it was for the best."

"You left me with them." I'm spitting my hate at my mother suddenly, flames bursting from my fingertips as I lash out verbally, my power wanting to strike her while my mind works through the truth. "All those years, knowing we were being manipulated and controlled. You let me work for them." I can't speak further, throat locked. Instead, I hammer my thighs with both fists, more tears coming, pouring down my cheeks, hot with flame, but out of rage. The fire begs to consume me, to carry me away from this agony, and I wish I could just let go and accept its offer.

"We couldn't take you out." My mother's voice is soft, but it reaches me, so full of anguish my own fury softens a little, enough I regain my focus, to pull back from temptation. "Zoe, if you'd seen what I've seen…"

she trails off, shaking her head, hands wringing before her. "There is a time and a place, my darling. For everything." She tries a little, wretched smile, eyes dark with hurt. "You of all should understand that."

I do. I'm an Oracle, just like her. I know fate works in mysterious ways. But I just can't work past the betrayal of my own mother abandoning me like this.

"Zo." Ash's tone is dark, but not harsh. "These people, they're family." She gestures behind her, my gaze drifting over the watchers. I recognize Helios bloodline markers in the women's dark hair and eyes. "Family working outside the sanctuary to protect the world from Belaisle and the Brotherhood."

The who? I shake my head, wiping at my tears.

"The sorcerers we work with," she gestures to Baird and a few others, "were once known as the Steam Union." Mother's words trigger memory.

"Piers?" I lick my dry lips. "Piers Southway. Do you know him?"

Baird grunts in anger when my mother appears confused. "The boy who's been hunting us."

Understanding lights her eyes. "No, dear one," she says. "This group are not of his kind. Though there was a time they had association with his people." Baird nods while my mother sighs. "This is no time for a history lesson. Just know the founder, Josephine Morrow, was unhappy with the way her people were headed and created our branch, moving out here to the coast." She opens her hands, gestures for the others to come forward. They do, though they stay at least three steps back, wariness in their eyes, the set of their bodies. "She was the first to uncover the sanctuary, to call on Oracles to join with her sect. And some of us did, interbreeding with the sorcerers in her care. This group has only ever been few in number, on purpose, their ultimate aim to protect the family."

"From the Brotherhood," Ash says. "Though, after the initial few left our people, the sorcerer sect cut off the Helios women from contact with the Steam Union, a fact we only just discovered shortly after you were born."

My mother's lips tighten. "I was restless. Spent my days wandering the city, much like you do, Zoe." She knows? She's been following me? "I was contacted," she says. "By Baird and his people." The big man grunts. "They had dwindled in numbers and in power, had lost their true purpose, though it was he who resurrected Josephine's true goal—to watch over the Oracles."

I shake my head, part of me fighting everything she says. "And yet," I say, flames beginning to stir, "you abandoned us. To the very people I take it you were supposed to protect us from." I bite back a curse. "For years, Mother. Years."

Ash's expression twists to sadness before returning to granite. "You're mother didn't abandon us, Zo. She escaped. And at great cost to her and risk to all of the family." I refuse to meet my mother's eyes, not caring what excuse is offered up. "She joined the Steam Union and started extracting some of our numbers to join her."

That makes me unwind a little, look around. I don't know any of the other faces. They must have left when I was small. Aunts, possibly? Cousins I've never met? And the men must be Steam Union.

"You know Liander and Sibyl are using our family for their own agenda." I glare at my mother, anger surging again, though this time it's not as all-encompassing and allows me to think, to process. "Why haven't you acted?"

Mother hesitates before speaking. "Because I can't," she says. "Not yet."

A vision, then, guides her. But she can't know what Liander is really doing. "He has a plan, to harm someone important." I shift my position, anxiety rising. This might be the chance to act, to save the family and stop Liander before he can act. "Mother, he's taking power from Gaia."

She shivers, hugs herself while the others sway a little. "I know," she whispers, the words carrying in the sudden silence on a sea-scented breeze. "And he plans to destroy a network of power so huge the repercussions will be felt by even the normals."

I gape at her as she just stands there. "And you're going to just let that happen?"

Agony and fear burn in her dark eyes as she raises her face to meet my gaze. "I have to."

No, this can't be happening. They have to help. Why else did Ash bring me here?

Mother turns away from me, chin dropping again, voice steady and calm. "Take her back, now, Ashtoria."

"Mother!" I lunge for her. This can't be right. But Ash stops me, one arm holding me back as my mother walks back toward the cottage door, the others following her with their eyes downcast. Only Baird glares at me while I stare open mouthed as they close the door behind them.

Ash lets me go, blue eyes unreadable. "I wanted you to know you're not alone."

A burst of temper flares, sparks flying from me as I shove her hard, backing away from her, letting my anger take over. Ash doesn't move, just watches me as I retreat.

"I wish you hadn't." I seize the fire within me and leap into the flames, the sound of her calling my name, her panicked face an afterimage behind my eyes.

The fire wants me and I am so tempted. It would be easier and cleaner and I could just let go. But if my deceptive mother and her useless friends won't help, I must at least try to offer a warning.

I leap from the flames onto a familiar beach and straight into his arms.

SEVENTEEN

Piers steps back a half pace, but keeps his grip on me as I tremble out my hurt and anger, looking up into his troubled gray eyes.

"What happened?" His British accent clips, words tumbling over themselves in his anxiety. Is it over my state or does he have his own dire news to share? "I tried to reach you when you called, but I just couldn't leave and missed you. I stayed, hoping you'd come back."

I gulp down my overload of emotions and the need to cry all over again, my hands rising and crossing over my chest to grip his which are still holding my arms tight. "I was afraid he'd attacked already and you weren't coming back."

His worry turns to serious concern, brows pulling together as Piers pulls me closer. "What are you talking about?"

"You have to help us." This time a sob does escape, more tears trickling down my cheeks, my face aching from all the crying I've done, the excess of emotion wearing at my strength. "If I tell you everything, will you save us?"

From ourselves. As powerful as I am, I can't go into the sanctuary alone. I need him to say yes.

Piers visibly calms, the tight grip on my arms softening, his face taking on deep kindness, such sincerity as I've never seen. For an instant, fear rockets to the surface. Everyone lies to me. Everyone. I've just had proof of that. And here I am, willing to trust Piers on the weight of a lifetime of visions that might or might not have been manipulated.

But he's not a stranger. I know Piers, I've felt his heart, felt my own, in the foresight I've lived and the times we've spent together. I know he's a good person, that his concern is real. And I have to trust someone.

"Just tell me," he says, lips descending to brush over my forehead, the faint scent of peppermint following the hot stroke of air as he speaks. "We'll figure it out together."

It takes little time to blurt my herky-jerky way through my story, though it feels like forever. He holds silent as I speak, though I can tell from the way his brow twitches, his lips moving a fraction, he has questions. Of course he does. I'm only giving him part of what he needs to know. But I fear we have no time for answers or a full disclosure of the history of my people, the pressure of the fire growing as each second passes. A vision is about to become manifest.

But which one?

Piers kisses me when I'm through, his skin cold compared to mine as the flames lick around the two of us. He gasps in a breath, but doesn't pull away, his sorcery smothering the fire before it can harm him. I sigh into his mouth, my sorcery connecting with his.

"I know the sorcerers you speak of," he says. "We've been seeking Liander Belaisle for a long time." Who does he mean by 'we'? It doesn't matter, though I'm certain Syd is among that number. "If you can show me where he's hiding, we can end this once and for all."

I nod quickly, hope a reality again. What do I need with Ash and my traitor mother? The tiny group of fearful ones who huddle together and don't act? Piers's determination is infectious, and I find myself smiling, eager.

He half turns, one hand releasing me, extending, as a black tunnel forms. I only have a moment to register the shock on his face and to realize he didn't create the tunnel.

And then we're surrounded by darkness deeper than any night, tunnels opening all around, black-robed men appearing to ring us in. Piers pulls me against him, one arm around me, his sorcery flowering out beneath him, but I know as he must, we're no match for so many. My gaze flashes over Kayden's snarl of jealousy as he stares at me in Piers's arms before I lock eyes with Liander.

"Hello, my boy." He smiles with nothing but contempt up at Piers. "I've been looking for you."

I can't let them take Piers. But the moment I reach for the flame, I'm smothered by a dozen back cloaks of power, my magic crushed under the gathered sorcerers while Piers's magic is devoured and he's driven to his knees.

He manages to look up, gray eyes full of pain, but he's smiling at Liander as the smaller man bends over him.

"Syd will be so happy to see you," Piers says.

Liander's smirk turns to fury, one hand lashing out across the younger man's face. Piers rocks sideways, spitting blood. But I see the fear in Liander, the way his eyes dart around the circle, hear the anxious note under his words as he speaks. "Take him." He kicks at Piers while Kayden and two others hurry forward, jerking Piers upright by his arms, their power smothering him. Liander turns on me, black drifting over his eyes. "As for you," he points a finger at me, "your grandmother won't be able to protect you this time."

I feel their hands on me before I know I'm surrounded, but it doesn't stop me from fighting. Again and again the fire tries to rise, the sorcerers cursing as flames lick them, only to be devoured again. I just need a little more time, but then we're in the tunnel and I'm falling into darkness.

They dump me onto the hard stone floor at Sibyl's feet, Liander appearing beside me a moment later. I look up into my grandmother's cold eyes and feel true hate for the first time in my life. Does she know my mother is alive? She must. And I will never forgive her for that.

"Your precious little brat was talking with the Steam Union." Liander's power jerks me to my feet, pushes me toward Sibyl. She catches me, her flames burning away his grip, but hers is no more gentle. It's only then I spot Rena peeking around her shoulder, glaring at me like I'm the enemy.

She has no idea what's really going on here, though I know just enough as it is, to put myself in harm's way.

"You foolish, foolish child." Sibyl's hand lashes out, the slap so loud my ears ring from it, my cheek on fire where her skin impacted mine. I stumble in her grip from the force of the blow, less staggered by the fact she's struck me than the fact my whole world is crumbling at the edges and I can't stop it. "How could you betray your own family like this?"

My jaw locks. I want to scream at her, to tell her what I know, but I hold my tongue. It's not going to make a bit of difference. I see her guilt, the subtle gleam of it in the back of her eyes, the way she wriggles against her own choices. She's fully aware and has been controlling and manipulating me and the rest of the family for a long time.

What visions have I missed because she's been holding me back?

"Kill her." Liander's spit travels almost the full distance between us, a sparkling drop arching from his lips.

Would my own grandmother really comply with such an order? For a moment, I fear she's lost to me, that he owns her completely. But the moment her shoulders stiffen and her jaw clenches, I know she might be duplicitous in his schemes, but she's not completely gone.

"Don't be ridiculous," she snaps. Liander's face turns deep red, a vein popping up in his forehead. But Sibyl speaks again before he can rupture something. "Zoe is my responsibility," she says, "and like it or not, we need her. She is the strongest of the Helios Oracles." His lips gape, protest almost visible as she turns to me. "However," she says, glaring down at me, hands fishing in my pocket, retrieving my lighter which she palms, "that power and your mind are clearly clouded by outside influence." I feel the flames in her mind press down on mine, her sorcery biting deep. I flinch from her touch, the scent of dying smoke passing through my nostrils as my fire sighs and retreats.

I start to shake, looking down at my hands, feeling inside myself for the flames so familiar. Nothing. Not even a coal remains, the life of it snuffed out. I look up into her eyes, trembling and teary-eyed as the magic that makes me who I am dies.

"It's not permanent." She touches my hair as though to reassure me, though it's the same hand that struck me only a moment ago, her other still clamped painfully around my arm. "I can reverse the effects if and when I choose." My knees want to buckle, to carry me to the floor, but I stay upright if only because of my grandmother's grip on my arm. I hear Rena's snigger, catch her wicked smile she covers with her chubby hands, but it doesn't matter. I hang there from Sibyl's strong hand as she arches an eyebrow at Liander. "Will that satisfy you for now?"

He glares at her a moment. "Keep an eye on her," he says. "I have other work to do."

I watch him leave, though only part of me is present. Everything has gone dull and gray, fuzzy at the periphery. The fire that lights my life is gone and I have no idea how to get it back.

EIGHTEEN

The moment Liander and his sorcerers leave, closing the door behind them, Sibyl releases her grip on me. I stagger to one side, away from her, hands rising to clasp my cheeks, an almost physical need to hold myself together pressing the palms and fingers tight against my own skin.

I shall start screaming at any moment and I'll never be able to stop.

"You had to act out now, of all times." Sibyl paces in front of me, anger cold and sharp. I can't speak, not yet, but I'm growing accustomed to this empty feeling, enough my own temper can rise. It's so wrong not to feel the fire join my anger, but that only makes my rage heat up worse.

"He's using us." I don't recognize my own voice. I

sound like an animal, a creature, not a girl. "He's draining power directly from Gaia." She spins on me, scowling. "But you knew that, didn't you, Grandmother?"

Rena suddenly looks less sure of herself while Sibyl snaps her fingers in my cousin's face.

"Out," she barks. Rena looks like she's going to protest, but one peek at my grandmother's face and she runs for the door. As soon as she's gone, Sibyl spins on me with a hiss.

"You're lying," she says, intensity in her eyes almost as animal as mine.

"I'm not." I still have access to my sorcery, but it's weak and thin. The fire feeds it, normally. Without sustenance, it's simply darkness looking for food. I let it go looking, skimming over my grandmother, under the floor, dragging her with me to the chamber below. To the main chapel and the altar.

Sibyl tries to pull away, but I can't allow her to retreat, not now. I touch the thread that is Liander and force my grandmother to feel it, too.

There is no shock in her, not really, telling me everything I need to know.

"You let him do this." I sag, releasing her. "Grandmother, how could you?"

She doesn't answer, or look at me. Neither of us moves for a long moment, not until the door opens and my aunt Ash walks through.

I'm shocked to see her, surprised enough it shakes me loose of the last of my despair over the absence of my power. Ash takes one look at me and scowls, stalking straight to Sibyl who tries to collect herself in time. Too late, she rocks back from Ash and the blow the younger Oracle delivers. My grandmother might have slapped me, but Ash isn't so careful, the punch strong enough to send Sibyl to the floor.

Instinct and training drive me forward, to my knees where I cradle my grandmother's head on my lap. She's stunned, suddenly sad, tears pooling in the corners of her eyes as Ash crouches next to her, shaking out her fist.

"You stupid old bitch," she says.

Sibyl's face hardens, her body stiffening as she struggles into a sitting position. Her power lashes out at Ash, who easily holds her back. Fire erupts between them, my aunt's calm demeanor level and flat while Sibyl hisses and writhes. When my grandmother collapses back again, I catch her, Ash shaking her head, lips twisted in contempt.

"Try that again," she snarls. "You're nothing without all of us and you know it."

My grandmother's hands flutter in her lap. "I've done my best for this family."

"You've lived like a parasite from this family," Ash says. "How old are you now, Grandmother? Four hundred? Five?" My aunt might as well have punched me, too. What is she talking about? "You just can't live with the fact we're outgrowing you in power. So you sold our souls to sorcerers to make sure you would never lose control." She snorts, stands, stares down at Sibyl like the woman in my arms is an insect she'd like to crush under her boot. "How's that working out for you, then?"

I don't know what I expected, the reaction I waited for, but the thin wail rising from Sibyl's chest wasn't it. I stare down at her with growing unease as her face crumples and she sobs once.

"I tried my best!" She's not convincing either Ash or me, and probably not herself. "I've led this family with honor and fortitude. Given up everything to ensure our survival." She jabs a shaking finger at Ash. "You should be grateful!"

Ash laughs in her face, a cold and horrible sound. "Grateful." Her eyes meet mine. "What about you, Zo? Feeling particularly grateful right now?"

I shake my head, pushing back away from Sibyl, letting her fall to the floor. I stand, circle toward my aunt, while my grandmother—or whoever she truly is to me— struggles to rise, her robes tripping her up.

"Behold," Ash says, arms crossing over her chest, "the mighty Sibyl, last of the Delphic Oracles. So power hungry and desperate she stole the magic of the Helios family who came after her to sustain her life and lead us far after her expiry date."

Sibyl manages to make it to her feet at last, gray hair coming loose from its perfect coil, a dark stain on the front of her white dress. "None of you would exist without me." She spits the words at us, a venomous old snake without the courage to strike.

Ash's magic crushes hers, drives her to her knees again. "I used to fear you." There is wonder in my aunt's voice. "We all did. Except Leyea."

"Do not speak her name in my presence." Sibyl's words don't hold the crackle they normally do.

"I only wish I'd believed her long before now. Had paid attention when she first came to me, told me what you were." Ash's arm drapes over my shoulders. "Did Zoe tell you?" She grins down at me. "They finally got to see each other again."

Sibyl wails one more time, groaning as she falls forward, forehead to the floor. "You will bring the end to us all."

"So you seem to think," Ash says. "Your precious vision of old, the one you claim keeps you in power. To prevent the destruction of the Helios Oracles." My aunt pauses, thoughtful. "Maybe it's time we were done, have you thought of that?"

Sibyl reaches out for me, eyes wild. "Don't listen to her, child. She is deceitful and wicked. She will encourage the last days of our family."

What does that mean? Fire singes me, flares in my

mind, and though I have no control or magic of my own, a vision forms—

—*You are chained, enslaved, thin and starving, your power spluttering as the laughing group of witches prod you and demand you show them their future, as though you are some parlor game to be played—*

"That is our future!" Sibyl's words drag me from the foretelling. "A life of slavery and waste."

I know better than to trust her, though there is real fear in the old woman's eyes. Ash doesn't give Sibyl a chance to keep talking.

"That is your future." Ash's brows are tight together, though she's still smiling. "Yours." I see it again, outside it this time, as Ash exposes the truth to me, her fire simmering with anger. She's right. It's not me at all. I see Sibyl's face clearly from this side of the vision. "And I believe you'll have earned it." Ash's arm tightens around me. "We're going now," she says. "And we're not coming back. Sibyl." She's suddenly serious, almost threatening. "If you come after us, I'll burn you in your own flames."

Sibyl just stares, sullen, broken. I pull Ash back as I reach for my power.

"She's taken my fire." I hurry to Sibyl's side, disgust spinning with growing hate as I search her dress and find my lighter in her pocket. Eyes locked on hers, I flip open the cap and turn the wheel. The instant the fire comes to life, I feel my magic return, flooding me with joyful, leaping flames.

I back away, Ash taking my hand and leading me to the door. We leave the wilting woman there on the floor, my aunt sealing it shut behind us. Her fire licks over the edges, sorcery molding to the seams.

"It won't hold her for long," Ash says, now in a hurry, hand on my elbow. "Once she pulls herself together, they'll be on us for sure."

I don't ask why we didn't just kill her, then, though I want to, savagery rising with the flames returned to me. "Where are we going?" We need to rescue Gaia, to break the control Liander has over her. But when I think suddenly of Piers, I gasp so loud Ash jumps. "They have him!" And, though guilt rides me, I feel the need to put him first.

Forgive me, my Goddess. He's a mere mortal and I love him.

Ash grins at me, jerking me around a corner and into shadowed nook. Her lighter is already out as we step inside.

"The handsome young sorcerer is a friend of yours, I take it?" She winks. "Feel up to a rescue?"

NINETEEN

My feet are heavy under me, dragging me down as Ash pulls me along behind her. Our short trip through the fire took us deeper under the earth, further beneath the sanctuary than I've ever been before. I had thought I'd explored most of it, only to discover just how wrong I've been.

I feel the presence of my family above me, their flames burning bright, though faintly through all the heavy rock. It's dark here, the air chill, rough walls slick with moisture and air scented with the tang of mildew. Ash seems to know her way around, at least. I'm guessing I'm not the only Helios to have explored this ancient place. And yet, this part of the sanctuary feels different, almost threatening. Partly because when I reach outward with my magic all I encounter is quiet, oppressive darkness.

I run into Ash as she comes to an abrupt halt, turning her head toward me to scowl at my clumsiness. I feel like a small child chastised for misbehaving and feel an instinctual pulling in, as though I can retreat into my own body and hide behind her. She pauses a moment at a T-intersection in the corridor, faint light coming from the left, more darkness to the right. My fingers twitch with the need to grasp the hem of her leather jacket and hold on, the haunted-house atmosphere raising the hairs on the backs of my arms.

Ash makes a soft, frustrated sound. "This way," she whispers, just as a large shape detaches from the depths of the right corridor and pounces on us.

At least, it feels that way, but it's only Rupe's shadow that descends across ours, his physical form skittering to a halt in front of my aunt. I have a fearful thought perhaps she isn't my aunt after all, even as she hisses at the damaged sorcerer.

"Away with you, pest," she says in a voice barely above a whisper.

He cackles in the darkness, right hand shifting into a malformed werewolf paw, two claws missing and the last digit twisted at an abnormal angle before it reverts to a human hand again.

"Go that way," he says. "If you want to get caught." His eyes turn to me, the faint light catching the moist corners, making me shiver.

Ash doesn't move, but she doesn't chase him off, either. "What do you know about it, freak?"

He snaps his teeth at her, spins away, circling her with hunched shoulders as he comes to my side. Ash follows him with her gaze, but makes no move to chase him off so I allow him to approach me, though the temptation to hide behind her is stronger still.

Pointed canines flash as he smiles at me, huge and gaping. "You want your boyfriend." He drags out the word in sing-song cynicism.

I nod, not bothering to argue Piers isn't my boyfriend.

Rupe wriggles like a puppy waiting to be petted. "I can show you, you know." His face contorts, from pain to ecstasy and back again so fast I wonder what's going on in his twisted head. "For a price."

Ash sighs, snaps her fingers in his face. He jerks away from her, one bare foot flaring into a giant wolf's paw, intact for once, save for the bald, weeping patches of skin that bubble ichor. I stare at it in horror as my aunt speaks.

"Why should we trust you?" She's absolutely correct. Rupe has been Liander's creature for as long as I've known him, even before he returned this damaged, broken thing before us. And yet, he showed me where to hide from the sorcerer, allowed me to eavesdrop with him on Liander and his plans. I hold up one hand to Ash and take a tentative step toward Rupe.

"Your price," I say, voice crackling a little, throat dry. "What is it?"

He hums a soft whine under his breath, dreadful paw returning to human shape. "Burn it out." His hands claw the air before me. "Burn out the wolf and I will help you."

I stare at him with pity and disgust fighting a pitched battle in my head. "I can't do that," I say. But Rupe is nodding over and over, panting as his snout extends and retracts.

"You can," he growls. "Burn it and I'll show you where he is."

Ash steps in before I can respond. "Take us to him first," she says, her own fire stirring, the air heating around her, driving Rupe back with a soft whine. "Then we'll see what we can do."

He bounces on his toes a few times, muttering to himself. I fear we're losing him and, pity winning, I reach out and touch his shoulder. He flinches from contact, but focuses on me with his upper lip arched in one corner, eyes narrowed.

"I promise," I say while Ash sighs heavily. "If you show me where Piers is, I'll do anything I can to help you." I glance at my aunt. "One more condition." Rupe waits, as does Ash. "You have to help us free him."

Rupe gnashes his teeth before turning away from me and, for a moment, I'm worried it's over and I was too late with my offer. But Rupe pauses on the lip of the dark entry to the right corridor and waves for us to follow.

Ash catches my arm, stopping me from going after him. "We can't trust him, Zo."

"I know," I say. "But he's helped me in the past. And I have to believe he'll do anything for his freedom."

She nods slowly, lets me go while Rupe pants and shakes his fists at us to hurry. "Fine," she says, taking the lead. "But one sign of betrayal and I'm putting his sorry ass out of his misery."

Somehow, I think he'd be grateful.

It takes a bit to get used to the darkness again after having the dim light at our disposal. I wish I could light a flame, but Ash seems confident enough and I hear Rupe shuffling ahead of us. My eyes finally adjust, heart pounding in my chest, and for the second time I run into the back of my aunt when she comes to a halt.

This time she doesn't react with anger, ignoring me completely in favor of something on the wall. I lean in around her shoulder and find Rupe hunched over, fingers rattling metal. When the small door opens, it's silent despite my worry it might creak, and I'm following Ash and the damaged sorcerer into a small room.

It's dark here, too, but only for a moment. Rupe crosses to the far wall, fingers reaching for a wooden slat. He slides it silently open, pressing his finger to his lips as though we need reminding to be silent. Two small holes shine light through and onto the back wall, bored through the stone and into the next room.

Ash leans in quickly, spending far too long in my opinion. I'm antsy, eager to see what's on the other side. But as she leans back, grim expression on her face, I catch the thin sound of a man screaming and I'm suddenly not so sure I want to look.

When I finally do, it's with clammy palms and an uneasy stomach threatening to do me in. I barely blink as I stare into the next room and gasp in shock and horror.

I'm not sure what I was expecting, but torture wasn't on the list. It's possible I'm simply naïve, or didn't consider Piers's worth to Liander. But as I stare through those peep holes at the bleeding, suffering form of the man I've loved in visions for most of my life, I receive an education in cruelty and evil.

They have him stretched out on a wooden slab, his hands over his head, bound like his feet with heavy leather straps. Two winches clack softly on either end, pulling him taut between them. They've stripped away his dress shirt, leaving his long, lean torso exposed, muscles straining against his bonds. Piers pants in heavy gasps as Liander stands over him, a metal rod heated to red hot at the tip, balanced in one gloved hand.

"How many are here with you?" The rod descends slowly, and only then do I see the row of marks along Piers's right side. His breathing speeds up, body twisting, trying to escape the torture, but he doesn't say a word. Not until the metal touches his flesh.

His scream drives me back, away from the peepholes, both hands slapping over my mouth to keep myself from answering Piers's shriek with my own. My stomach boils, tries to overflow, but I swallow it down and hold myself rigid, immobile, while the wave of nausea and overwhelm passes.

Ash grabs my arm and jerks me back toward the door, Rupe trailing along behind us. It's not until the three of us stand in the corridor, the door closed again, that she grasps the sorcerer by the front of his shirt and slams him physically into the wall so hard the thud of contact and the whoosh of his outward breath makes me worry she might have done some permanent damage.

I reach for her to stop her, but she's in Rupe's face.

"Tell us what Liander is up to." She shakes Rupe while he squirms to escape her. I remember him as a tall, strong young man, back before he left us. But the wolf in him has affected change, and not for the better. He's skinny, and no match for her, it seems.

"I don't know." He turns his head away, sulky look on his face.

"You mean you won't tell me." Ash pulls him back and shoves him into the stone again. Rupe protests with a snarl, but no amount of wriggling wins his freedom. "It doesn't matter now." She lets him go, wiping her hands on her leather pants. "I should just get you out of here, Zo. But I can't let that boy die."

Considering I'm not leaving without him, Ash has made the right decision.

I turn to Rupe, offering my hand—

—you're in the dark, outside it, looking in. And she's there, in the distance, standing in the back yard of a tall, white house, looking at you in confusion. You have to reach her, but it's too late, the darkness is coming for her, it has her surrounded, is devouring her while the hundred souls who look to her scream her name and fall into the abyss—

—flames erupt, a field of fire, stakes towering into the night, bodies burning, she's burning, screaming while her rainbow magic rises to the stars—

I cough out a breath I've been holding for too long and draw a long, shaking pull of air. Rupe stares at me, eyes huge, hands trembling while I fight to recover from the vision. It's like nothing I've ever experienced before, so immediate I'm trembling all over, fear overpowering as I turn to Ash.

Rupe scrambles off and I let him, though Ash curses after him. She takes one look at me and her anger dissolves into fear of her own.

"We have to save her." I clutch at my aunt's hands as she supports me. "The darkness is coming for her and she has no idea."

TWENTY

We barely make it two steps when I'm taken by the flames again—

—*a woman bends over Gaia, the rainbow shielding around the Goddess gone, the woman's face turning toward you, smiling at you, beckoning you—*

I miss a step and bang my nose on Ash's shoulder. She spins and catches me while I gasp for air.

"Gaia." Ash's eyes tighten, her lips thinning as I shudder from the power of the vision. "She's in trouble."

My aunt doesn't seem as concerned as she should be, tsking softly as she seems to weigh our options. I shove her gently, enough to get her attention.

"We have to save her." The urge to protect Piers first fades as the vision repeats itself. Whoever the woman was, I've seen her before. And the source of the vision is happening now, right now, at this moment. While Syd's fate is imminent, Piers's just as intense, I'm certain they both have more time than Gaia.

Ash shoves me back, but softly, almost kindly. "Go then," she says. "I'll take care of the boy. If you think it's necessary."

I gape at her. "She's our Goddess."

My aunt shakes her head, but doesn't respond. She simply turns and leaves me there in the dark, rapidly lost to my sight. I almost go after her, a terrible fear growing in my soul, one last blow, one final lie I don't know if I can face. But I can't let any further harm come to Gaia.

My lighter is in my pocket and I reach for it, flipping open the top, looking down into the flame I strike. It dances and sways, beckoning me inward, though I am now afraid of what it means. I close my eyes and tumble into the fire, focused on the altar and my Goddess.

I'm there before I can blink away the wisp of smoke created by the single flame, feet touching down on stone as I stare at the scene before me.

I was right—this vision wasn't so much a premonition as a warning of what is happening right now, in this moment. The woman straightens from where she leans over Gaia, a soft smile on her face. I sense no guile in her, or deceit, but I've been lied to so long, by so many people, I call the flames anyway, just in case.

It's so strange to see Gaia's face laid bare, unprotected

by the rainbow shielding. Her eyes remain closed, though, her hands folded yet over her breast. I look up from careful examination to ensure my Goddess is all right and into the strange woman's face.

It takes me a moment to realize she looks familiar, and why that is. Even as my gaze flickers to Gaia and back to the woman again, I feel my jaw drop and my heart skip a beat before pounding back into painful life.

"Zoe Helios." She knows my name, her soft, kind voice carrying to me in the quiet of the chapel. The fire dies in me, goes quiet, listening to her as she speaks. "I want to thank you for helping me find my sister." She beckons to me, holding out one hand. "Come closer," she says. "I want you to see what you've done."

She doesn't seem angry or feel antagonistic, but I hesitate, awe and wonder slowing my steps though I obey her without thought. "You." I breathe in, breathe out as I approach, mind skipping. "You're Gaia's sister." How can this be? A living Goddess, standing before me, another sleeping at her feet, and I'm about to take her hand.

Her skin is smooth, soft, warm. It feels human, which makes me shudder from her touch, though she won't let me go, pulling me toward her. I stand, shaking and lost, looking down at my Goddess while her sister tucks me against her side and kisses my temple. Her long, blonde braid brushes my bare arm, hangs to my feet, the scent of her like coffee and warm cookies on a Sunday afternoon.

"My Goddess," I whisper.

The woman frowns, shakes her head. "I'm afraid not," she says. "Far from it, in fact." She sighs, releases me, and sinks to her knees beside Gaia. I almost fall as my body folds downward, joining her on the stone. "I'm just a woman," she says, touching Gaia's face with one hand. "Well, not quite." Good humor twinkles in her eyes as she meets mine. "But a Goddess? Not me."

"But..." I stammer, my brain stuttering over the truth, believing her as the last of my life's lies falls apart around me. "Gaia."

The woman nods. "She is like me," she says. "No more a Goddess than you are, Zoe." She sighs. "My name is Iepa. We are maji. And I've been looking for my sister for a very long time."

"NO!" We're not alone. I had no idea Sibyl was here, though from the disheveled look of her she's only just arrived. She stares at Iepa with huge, frightened eyes. "What have you done?"

The maji woman's kind expression turns cold. "I could ask you the same question." Her hand rises, her power pinning Sibyl, dragging her down to force her to sit on one of the benches, ropes of rainbow light holding her tight. Sibyl squirms a moment, face twisting from anger to loathing to despair.

I ignore her, trusting Iepa to keep her contained, as I've trusted no one else in my life. I have no idea what she's talking about, but I know in my heart she's telling me the truth. Iepa holds my hand, keeps her grip on me as she gazes with sadness down on Gaia. I reach out slowly, touch the soft, pale skin of the woman I believed to be my Goddess as her sister speaks.

"She's been missing for centuries," Iepa says. "But no one else would help me look for her, and the Universe is so vast." She squeezes my hand, sits back to wipe a tear from her cheek with her free hand. "I searched everywhere for her, feared her dead. It wasn't until I felt her through you only last night I realized she was being shielded from discovery."

I'm numb and cold, but that doesn't stop me from speaking. "Liander Belaisle," I say. "And the Brotherhood." That's what Piers called them, isn't it?

Iepa nods. "Indeed," she says.

"You've betrayed us all, Zoe!" Iepa's magic might hold Sibyl still, but she's done nothing to silence the woman.

I lick my dry lips, wishing I could just forget all of this, go back to the ignorance of two years ago. But even as I do, I shake off my apathy and the frozen state I've fallen into, letting the fire rise to cleanse me and free me from my grief. "If not a goddess," I say. "If a maji, then for what purpose?"

Iepa smiles. "Must we have a purpose?" I don't smile back and she finally shrugs. "We are hands of the

Creator," she says. "But so are you, Zoe."

"But she is our Goddess." I shiver, rub my arms after releasing Iepa's hand. "The source of our foresight." That's what I was taught.

"No, child." Iepa's sad eyes tell me everything I need to know. "Gaia is nothing of the sort."

"Liar!" We both turn at the wailing sound of Sibyl's denial. She's weeping openly, her fire licking through the coils of rainbow light. "She is a Goddess!"

Iepa rolls her shoulders in a shrug. "I do believe she did nurture your talent when your family's particular power appeared on this plane." She frowns, shakes her head. "I should have thought to check here, I suppose, but she gave up on guiding you so long ago, I thought her elsewhere." She smooths her braid with one hand. "More the fool I," she says. "Doing so must have exposed her to the Brotherhood and offered them the means to capture and contain her."

"And take her power." I flinch as Iepa looks up, darkness on her beautiful face. I'm having trouble assessing her age, she feels timeless to me.

"Correct." She now sounds angry, though I know her fury isn't aimed at me. She looks over my shoulder, glaring at Sibyl who has fallen still. "Tell me, betrayer of your blood—how did they manage it, then, those most foul of sorcerers? Gaia is," her lips tighten as she corrects herself, "was one of the strongest of us. A mere human sorcerer should not have been able to contain her."

Sibyl turns her face away, jaw tight. But Iepa isn't willing to accept her silence. The maji woman leaps to her feet and sweeps toward the old Oracle who shudders from her.

"Don't touch me!" She leans away, writhing as though Iepa's skin is diseased. The maji clamps one hand over Sibyl's shoulder and squeezes enough her knuckles whiten. Her face twists as Sibyl shudders and finally sags under the pressure of a flow of rainbow magic that seems to sizzle against the old woman's fire.

"Enough!" Sibyl sobs the word and Iepa releases her. I shiver as Sibyl weeps, tears gathering under her chin. "It was me. I lured Gaia to me, fed her poisoned wine." Spite enters her tone, an old evil I've never seen before rippling across her face. "They offered me power and I took it, for all of us." She meets my eyes, desperate all over again. "For the family, Zoe. For you!"

I turn away from her as Iepa slowly makes her way back to me, sitting at her sister's side. "Treachery," she says. "She trusted you, Sibyl. Spoke highly of your family. Clearly, she was much more naïve than I thought to fall for such a trap."

"They were strong," Sibyl whispers. "And she was weak."

"More likely," Iepa says, "your betrayal broke her heart and spirit." Iepa sighs, turns away and again touches her sister's face, a tiny sparkle of rainbow light traveling between them. "And, ever since, the Brotherhood has been using her as a power source, likely all these centuries. Feeding from her." Iepa's jaw tightens. "Until there is so little left of her there is nothing remaining to save."

Tears well in my eyes at her words, my chest tight with sudden grief. My fire reaches out for Gaia and the moment my power makes contact, I feel the truth. "She's dying."

Iepa nods slowly, head bobbing as tears splash on her sister's cheek. "She is."

I sit back, weeping for her loss though she remains yet, breath rhythmic, chest rising slowly and steadily. I need to leave, to escape this horror, but Iepa doesn't move and I can't bring myself to leave her there.

"Terrible things are coming." I don't know if Iepa cares or can help, but I need to tell someone. "Darkness, fire, death."

She looks up slowly, meets my eyes. "Tell me what you've seen."

I do, including my most recent vision, about Syd, the stakes, and her death. I'm certain the rise of her rainbow power means she's about to die.

"That's what he's been after." Rage flickers over Iepa's face, makes her look fierce and powerful for a moment where once grief kept her small. Her gaze returns to her silent sister, fists clenching at her sides. "Gaia is almost drained. He's known her end is coming and has been looking for a replacement, a way to fill her role. For more power to steal for his damned Brotherhood." She looks away from her sister, away from me, staring at the stone floor. "He hasn't been trying to kill Syd. He's been trying to capture her."

"Why?" I know the answer even as I speak it. Haven't I seen it enough times? The iridescence, the same as Gaia's, as Iepa's. I made the connection not too long ago Syd's magic looked like my Goddess's. Does that mean she's maji?

Iepa turns back, jaw set, eyes flashing rainbow fire. "They have to listen now," she says, though I'm certain she's not speaking to me. "The Brotherhood has crossed the line, stealing power from the maji this way." She stands and I rise with her, though she doesn't move to leave, just hovers there over her sleeping sister. "Surely they will finally act, if only out of self-preservation."

I have no idea who she's talking about, but I can't let her leave if that's her plan. "What of Gaia?" Now I know the truth, my heart breaks for the slumbering woman in the gold-gilt coffin.

Iepa bites her lower lip, shaking her head. "There is nothing to be done." She barely speaks above a whisper. "My sister is too far gone for me to reach. Only the last echo of her remains, keeping her body alive. When that is gone, all which made her who she is will be lost." She turns on me, suddenly fierce, grasping my arms in her hands, shaking me slightly. "Listen to me, Zoe Helios," she says. "Your people are on the wrong path."

I nod. I know that already.

"There is a war coming." Iepa sounds afraid, though her intensity doesn't fade, nor her feeling of rebellion. I wonder who she has need to defy and if she's much like me, in the end. "You must be on the right side." She shudders, steps away. "I have a terrible feeling we might need you before this is done."

"I won't fail you." I don't know why it's important she know I'm with her, or that she know I'm loyal to the visions her sister's power encouraged all those years ago. But it is, to me.

Iepa smiles a little, body stiff, hands clenched at her sides again as she begins to glow with rainbow light. A tear forms in the very air next to her, a gash in the fabric of the plane, gushing bright light through it as she turns and brushes her hands over it. "You owe me nothing," Iepa says. "Just promise me, when the time comes, you'll do what you can to save her."

I look down at Gaia, confused, but Iepa is shaking her head.

"Syd," she says. "No matter what it takes, Zoe. Save Syd." And then, she's gone.

The sudden dimness makes my eyes water, the quiet

enveloping me as I draw a deep breath and let it out again. My grandmother doesn't move from where Iepa pinned her though the rainbow light fades and frees her. I briefly wonder if Iepa's bald speaking of truth has broken the old woman at last. Though now I hardly care.

Instead, I crouch and brace myself on the sides of Gaia's tomb before placing a kiss on her cheek. The barest sigh escapes her as my power connects with what is left of her.

"I'm so sorry." One of my tears falls to her face and I brush it away. "I wish I could have saved you."

Her lips part as I stare down at her, a sparkling trail rising from her mouth as she exhales for the last time. The shimmering breath rises to greet me, slipping into my nostrils, my own open mouth, the corners of my eyes. I shiver as the remains of Gaia's power sparks on my skin before racing through me, into me, melding firmly with my own magic.

Wonder and awe hold me still as I warm inside from the soft presence of her. And then, she's gone and the power is mine. I bend and kiss her one last time, before rising, turning, leaving the remains of whom she was behind.

And face down Sibyl as she snarls at me and throws flame in my face.

TWENTY-ONE

I brush away the fire with one hand, contempt for the woman before me burning harsher than any blaze she can send my way. She staggers a little, eyes huge as her power is deflected.

"Zoe." She holds out one hand to me, face morphing from shock to the old arrogance I'm so used to. But her fear is palpable now, and I wonder if she's always been afraid of me. "You can't believe a word that woman told you."

"And yet," I say as I descend from the altar and approach the woman I thought my grandmother, "I do, Sibyl. You, on the other hand." I flick flame at her, feeling a burst of satisfied vengeance as Sibyl swats at them with shaking fingers. "You have been lying to me my entire life." Our entire existence hangs in the balance of this discovery. Who my family are, what our power is really for, has been hidden from us, disguised and masked by outside force for centuries. I have no idea what will become of us, but for the first time we will be free to grow and understand our purpose.

If we get the chance.

"I've done everything I could to protect you." A thin wail hides behind her brashness. "I've sacrificed my own happiness for this family, long before you were born."

"Why, Sibyl?" I'm tired of her, just want her to go away. I have work to do. But I can't help but ask. "Why did you sell us out to the Brotherhood?" Surely not just for power. We have more than enough of that, the flames an endless source of fuel for us.

She flinches back as though I've slapped her. "She abandoned us, Zoe." Hateful spite spits from her lips as the heart of the truth comes out, faint madness in her eyes. I see all her years pile down on top of her as she strikes with words at the empty shell over my shoulder. "All those centuries she guided us, my mother, my mother's mother. From the beginning." She shudders, eyes moist, lips twisting with sorrow. "And then she left us." She hunches forward, an ugly sob escaping. "She abandoned me!"

Now I understand the real way of it at last. "Gaia tried to move on," I say. "And you hated her for it."

"How could she leave me?" Sibyl reaches for me, falls to her knees when I step back out of her range. She paws at my jeans with desperate hands. "Yes, I hated her." She spits, mood shifting to bitterness. "My visions were strong with her, don't you understand? But when she left, I was weak." She sinks to her hip, defeated. "We were all weak."

"So you laid a trap for her." The desire to kill Sibyl is so powerful I sway from the effort it takes to hold my ground. "You made a pact with the Brotherhood."

"I had no choice." Her voice is soft, empty. "Gaia left me and they offered me power. In exchange for her."

My hands ache from the fists they've made at my sides, my fire begging me to strike her down. She looks up at me then, so pathetic, so worthless, I can't be bothered. She's not worth the flame it would take to kill her.

"You're done lying to my family," I say, stepping around her. "When this is over, I'll make sure you answer for this, Sibyl." In a flash of insight, I recall what she'd done to me. I go to her, search her robes while her hands flap at me, slapping my skin though I continue, grim against such a pathetic onslaught, until I liberate the shining gold lighter tucked into her cleavage.

The top rings as I flip it open, flame leaping to life when the wheel spins. I focus all of my power on it, on her, and feel the draw of her magic as I douse her fire and cut her off.

The rush of power is almost staggering. I almost didn't expect it to work. Sibyl stares at me a moment, aghast, sheet-white and shaking. Before collapsing face first to the floor and clawing at the stone.

And I leave her there, weeping uncontrollably in the presence of the maji she betrayed. I hope she chokes on her tears.

I don't notice I'm not alone until I'm almost at the door, only then spotting Ash. She's leaning with her back against one of the Gaia statues, watching me with careful eyes. I approach her, hug her and welcome her returned embrace.

"How much did you know?" There's nothing accusatory in my tone. I'm really curious. All of my anger has been burned away by the fire inside me.

"Some," Ash says, voice thick. She's more worked up about this than I thought. "Not enough, apparently." She wipes at her nose with the side of her hand, eyes bright with moisture. "Let me kill her, won't you?"

Like she needs my permission for anything. But the way she watches me, the way Ash waits, tells me something's changed. I shake my head, looping my arm through hers, leading her to the door.

"Let her suffer without her power," I say. "For a little while. Let her know how Gaia felt." If Gaia truly even felt anything. "I want her to truly understand what she's done, what the price of her power hunger has been." Ash nods, grins a vicious grin. I wish I could muster some vindictiveness, but my need for Sibyl to feel her failure comes from a pure sense of justice. "I'll return for her later, when she's seen the error of her ways. Now, tell me you've rescued Piers and we can get out of here."

"Not yet," Ash says. "They moved him from the torture room. But I know where he is."

That's the first good news I've had all night.

I almost stumble over Rena as Ash and I exit the chapel. My cousin's stormy expression tells me I'm in for an earful, but I don't have time for her dramatics. She grasps my arm, pulls me to a halt, even as my aunt moves to block her. I wave Ash off and face down Rena as the younger Oracle plants her free hand on her hip and glares at me.

"What were you doing in the chapel?" She's cocky, bossy. Clearly Sibyl has given her some reason to feel superior to me for her to act this way. I recall the suppression of my power and grin in Rena's face. It's not her fault, nor should I take any of this out on her, but the fire calls to me, is angry and ready to fight. And Rena is a clear target.

I let it out to flare around me, watch as her eyes flash from contemptuous to shocked. She drops her hand from my arm with a tiny squeal of anguish, looking down at her smoking fingers before meeting my eyes again.

"Grandmother is going to be so mad at you." There was a time, not so long ago, I thought Rena loved me, was my friend as well as my blood. But now I see the deep-seated spite in her, the way her envy has eaten at her through her entire life, turned her against me. She's just like Sibyl. "I'm telling."

Rage like I've never known washes away the remnants of my loyalty to Rena, and through her, to my family. I step into her space, bending over her, nose almost touching hers as I smile with my teeth bared and slap her with fire.

Rena shrieks and spins, running for her life, feet slapping the stones as she goes. I know her distress will bring curious onlookers, despite the lateness—or is that earliness by now—of the hour. But it was worth it.

Ash rolls her eyes at me, takes my wrist in her hand, opening the top of her lighter.

"If you're done playing." But there's a twinkle back in her eye and for the first time since this started I feel optimistic things really might work out after all.

As I step into her flame, I feel the tingle of the remains of Gaia's magic work its way through my system, burrowing deeper inside me. It's mine, without a trace of her consciousness tied to it, but it feels different. It is altering me as it makes itself at home. Even the pleading flame seems subdued, curious about this new phenomenon and leaves me be. When I exit the flame with Ash at my side, I'm the most calm and focused I've been in a very long time.

Two sorcerers stare at us as we approach and I realize we're below the main sanctuary again. Ash's hips take on a decided wiggle, her eyebrow arching, a sultry smile bending her full mouth. I watch with surprise as she sashays to the young men, exuding sex appeal, her fire power tuned up to maximum effect.

The results are predictable. She is a stunning woman, no matter she has a decade on the two, and they both relax and grin at her as she joins them. I approach more slowly, certain I could never repeat her performance, and am just in time to catch the first as he crumples, shock on his face just before his eyes roll back in his head and he slumps sideways. He's heavy and almost carries me down with him, but I manage to ease him to the floor with a hearty grunt. The second is already on his way down, though Ash just lets him fall with a disdainful toss of her blonde hair.

"This way." She pushes through the iron gate, the squeal of unoiled hinges making me grind my teeth. I hurry after her, eyes flashing left and right, searching the plain, empty cells on either side of the short corridor. The stink of old urine and sweat mixes with a hint of rot and I swallow past my imagination's stirrings of what could cause such a stink. All of that goes away the moment I reach the last cell and my eyes settle on a beloved face.

"We don't have much time." Ash's hand rises, her lighter held toward the main door of the cell block. "Liander will have felt the attack on his sorcerers." And the passing of Gaia, surely. I hadn't thought of that. "I'll hold them off when they come, but you have to get him out of there."

It only takes me a moment to understand why. As I rush to the bars, place my hands on them, I feel the sticky, sucking power of sorcery as it tries to pull my strength out of me. I turn to Ash, but the distant sound of footsteps, coming fast, spins me back to Piers.

"Wake up." I toss a pebble at him, bouncing it from his narrow chest. He groans softly, rolls over on his side, one gray eye cracking open. It's bloodshot, and it takes him a moment to focus, but when he finally does, he smiles a lop-sided grin and waggles his fingers at me.

"Heya, Zo," he says, voice high-pitched and wobbly.

I grit my teeth and rattle his bars, acutely aware of the sound of danger getting closer. Ash hisses at me while I test the power around the cell with my own. It tries to pull in my fire and I can only imagine it's keeping Piers nice and docile. But even as my mind grapples with a plan, Piers sits up slowly, shaking his head, coming into focus.

"Don't do it." He holds up one trembling hand, the other pressed to his forehead. "If you try to come in, Belaisle's power will just trap you, too."

My aunt lets out a curse and runs down the cell block. I hear her retreat, feel the soft displacement of air and the whoosh of flame as she attacks someone. This is wrong, I need to fight with her, but she's giving me the chance to free Piers and I can't waste it.

I reach through the bars, the slick feeling of the shielding sliding over my skin like a glove. "Take my hand."

He shakes his head. "Just leave me, Zoe," he says. "Go warn Syd."

Doesn't he understand I can't abandon him here? "I need you." The words grunt from me as I push harder against the shield. Is it giving, just a little bit? I call up flame, contain it in my own sorcery, black flames eating at the wards. A shiver of sizzling sparks bursts, the new power inside me waking and answering the call. It knows this magic keeping me from Piers, knows it intimately. It's been unable to fight against the power, which kept it prisoner, that siphoned it to death.

That is, until now. I let it loose, tied to my fire, and feel the flames roar forth. Black fire bursts before me, devouring the power holding Piers at bay. I can feel him in it, feel it eating him alive and, with a snarl of rage at the defilement, I sever the connection and throw all of his power back to him.

Piers rocks on his hips, eyes coated black a moment before his head snaps forward, lips tight and grim. He leaps to his feet, wincing and hugging his damaged side, but he's alive and powerful again. And free.

The flames want to live on, but I smother them, stuffing them down, and they finally retreat, sulky, angry. I've never felt them this way before, with darkness wound through them and I wonder what I've done freeing Piers from his prison.

He comes to me, grasps my hand, the way now open for him. I look up the hall, catch sight of Ash retreating at a run, blackness reaching for her and throw out flame in her path. She vanishes into it, heading for I don't know where, but at least she's free. Liander appears through the wisps of smoke that remain, running for me with a shout on his lips, Kayden at his side, but they are too late. I see him clearly now, as the thief and liar he is, the weakling standing on the shoulders of others. A parasite, with no true power of his own, the real curse of the Brotherhood. I point at him with grim intent at the same instant I flare with fire and take Piers with me into the blaze.

TWENTY-TWO

This ride through the flames feels off, different, the heat burning me, dragging me down with need and hunger as powerful as that of the sorcery that held Piers. I realize my mistake almost too late. I've absorbed some of Liander's magic, taken into me that which I've come to despise and it is fighting me for control.

Is this how it feels to be one of them? How can they live with themselves? I battle the urge to devour everything, to emerge from the fire and feed and feed until the entire world dies. This is wrong, so wrong, and yet it feels like a dream I wish I could live forever.

Sparks sizzle and pop, sliding along the edges of the black, burning it away, sending it scrambling, trying to escape as the fire I've come to know roars and crackles and eats the sorcery alive. The power that was Gaia surges inside me, pushing back the black, finally crushing it as I grasp tight to Piers and hurl us from the flames.

I wake in a cool room, a soft breeze washing over me from an open patio door. White, gauzy curtains flap gently over the end of the bed, crisp sheets scented with lemon and the aroma of a summer's night. Something warm and firm lies under my cheek, my hand, and I open my eyes to find I've been using Piers's bare chest as a pillow.

I don't want to move. It would be lovely to savor this moment, but I as I lift my head and look out into the sunset of evening, I realize I've lost most of the day. We're out of time to stop the Brotherhood, to save Syd as I promised Iepa I would. Or are we? Disorientation and lost hours make me slightly woozy. I tip my head, look up to find Piers smiling at me, hand rising to slip through my hair and all of my worry goes away, if only for a moment.

He bends his long neck, kisses me, silken hair brushing my cheek. He feels strong again, and as my hands travel over his ribs, healed and whole.

"What happened?" I sit up, find myself still dressed in my T-shirt and jeans. Someone tucked us into bed, it seems.

"You saved my skinny behind," he says, voice amused, though threads of worry remain.

I shiver, slipping from the bed, thinking of Ash. "Has

my aunt showed up?" Where did I send her? Where am I? Was she able to grasp the fire I offered and make her own destination? I wasn't even thinking, just needed to give her a way out. I have no idea if she was even able to use my flame.

Piers climbs out of bed himself, slips on a long-sleeved shirt, long fingers making short work of the buttons. "I don't know," he says. "Let's go find out."

Haste and anxiety push me to keep going, though I'm weary, so tired and ready for this to be over. And it will be, soon, if my visions are correct. If I'm wrong we're too late, if haven't already missed my window. This could already be over and I don't even know it.

When I emerge from the bedroom, it's with such speed I almost collide with a beautiful, dark skinned woman who lets out a small shriek as I pull to a halt just in time. She grasps my shoulder in one hand with a quick exhale, smiling up at Piers who grasps her in his arms and hugs her tight.

"Tallah." He lets her go. "How did you find us?"

"The message you sent was clear enough," she says, eyes locked on me. "You've been here for hours. I was just coming to see if I could wake you."

I wish she'd come sooner.

Piers performs the introductions, while Tallah shakes my hand. I feel power in her and know before he tells me she's a witch. I'm soon seated at her kitchen counter with a cup of hot coffee in my anxious hands while a small group of her coven join us. They watch and listen as Piers fills them in on the little he knows, guesses mostly I can only assume he gleaned from the questions Liander asked him during his torture. Finally he turns to me when he runs out of things to say.

I'm tongue tied, nervous, just want to hurry up and go after Liander before he can enact his plan. But worse, I can't do it alone. How much can I trust them? I'm still hesitant, urgency a harsh counter point, when Piers takes my hand.

"It's okay," he says. "They love Syd."

Syd. Just the sound of her name makes me tremble, the flames pushing forward, the intensity of the vision so close I know we're almost out of time. "She's in danger." I don't mean to blurt, but the words escape before I can stop them. Tallah nods, grim faced.

"I've been trying to reach her." She gestures behind her. "We all have. With no luck."

Piers frowns, hand tight on mine. "Did you try going to Wilding Springs directly?"

Tallah nods, the woman beside her bobbing her head in time, short, black hair shiny in the lights of the kitchen.

"Several times." She looks at Tallah.

"Anna and I both went," Tallah says, full mouth tight with worry. "It's like when we try to travel, we get bounced back."

"Erica?" I have no idea who that is, but Tallah just grunts and shrugs.

"I've been trying to reach her, too," she says, voice sharp. "But our esteemed Council Leader is unavailable."

That sounds very bad to me. And reminds me of one of my visions. "Is she blonde?" A sick feeling jabs me in the stomach. "At Harvard?"

Tallah stares at me like I've grown a second head, and I want to scream at her to pay attention. "Erica Plower," she says. "The Leader of the North American Witches Council. And yes, her office is at Harvard."

I lean forward, grasp her hand, my fingers digging into her flesh. "Listen to me," I say, panic almost winning, making it hard to focus as everything slides into place. All my visions coming together into a whole that brings terror to my heart. While I can't trust what I've seen, I am certain Liander's guidance of the seeking from the night before was accurate. He wouldn't deceive himself, after all. "You can't trust her any longer. And if Liander is allowed to complete his plan, there will be terrible consequences." Fire and blood and death. I now understand the stakes, the flames. Witches, burning. Iepa's warning about a war coming.

Tallah's face pales, goes gray. I release her, the blaze inside me rising, surging, fighting for control. I push back from the counter, the stool I sat on crashing to the floor behind me, but no one moves to help, to touch me.

Smoke rises from my skin, my vision turning gold around the edges as the fire tries to drag me under.

Only the steady, supportive stare of Piers's gray eyes holds me here. I latch onto him, to his power, use him as a lifeline as my whole being tries to burn up. His sorcery doesn't feed from me, but holds me steady, encapsulates and insulates me until I can finally, painfully, crush the magic inside me and regain control.

I bend in half as it eases off, mouth open, panting air into my lungs. "Something is wrong," I whisper, though I don't know if anyone hears but me.

Tallah lurches to her feet, blue fire flaring around her. "I'm getting to the bottom of this once and for all," she says. As her power flickers and goes out.

She stares at her hands a long moment, shock on her face so genuine I feel terrible for her.

"Tallah." Anna joins her, feeds her power, but with the same result. I feel their magic leaving them, and choke on the truth.

"It's too late," I say, doing my best not to let them hear the wail building in my head. "He's already begun."

They stare at me with growing horror.

"He has." My mother steps through the open patio doors and meets my eyes, her small band of rebels behind her. "And we have little time if we want to stop him."

Tallah and her people react protectively, but their power seems to fizzle out as they try to shield themselves.

The coven leader's distress is obvious, though Piers puts himself physically between me and my mother as Baird steps forward, antagonism so clear in his body language I'm sure everyone in the room feels threatened.

"Where is Ash?" It's his only question and makes me wonder what their connection might be. I push past Piers, beyond worrying about Baird and the others not liking me, my whole focus on my mom.

"What's happening?" Tallah's hands are shaking, her people gathering around her. My mother's grim expression worries me even more. "Why can't we use our magic?"

My mother shrugs. "Liander's plan," she says, like that explains everything. "I'm sorry, but there's nothing we can do for you. Zoe." She turns to me like they aren't in the room, like we're not standing in Tallah's house. My mother's casual wave dismisses the danger the witches are in while my heart clenches against her. "We need to go before it's too late."

"It's already too late," I snap at her. "If he's started what he set out to do, we need to find a way to stop him."

She shakes her head, stubbornness in her dark eyes. I look very much like her, though time and worry have worn lines around my mother's lips and furrowed her brow, threading sparkling silver through her hair. "I have seen it," she says, as though we're the only two people in the room. "Years ago, Zoe. The time has come. And no one matters, nothing matters. But you."

I feel the animosity of the group she's brought, look up to see Baird glaring at me with hateful eyes. Is this why they despise me, why they fear me? Some foresight my mother had so long ago it could have changed course well before now?

But when I turn back to her, I see the conviction in my mother's gaze, the way she stares at me. I know what that look means.

"How many times have you had the same vision?" It's a hard question to ask.

"More times than I can remember," she says, voice steady, level, hand reaching out to me. "And if you don't come with me right now, Zoe, it will come to pass."

"What is it?" I must know. I can't just walk out of here, abandon these people who have tried to help me, not without understanding everything.

Mother hesitates, but Baird's voice crackles through our mutual silence. "Show her," he rumbles. "And let's finally be free of this, Leyea."

Her power opens to me and I seize her flames. My mother flinches, eyes wide, as I take control of her magic and force myself into her mind. I don't mean to be cruel or hurtful, but I'm tired of being lied to, of being told part of what I need to know. She surrenders to me as I dig deep for the vision—

FORESIGHT

—You stand over her dying body, Syd crumpled and empty, as she withers in the flame, your power engulfing the entire world, drawing on all the magic around you, until you rise, flaring into giant being, and consume the world—
—But even as it happens, this vision shifts, adjusts, shimmers at the edges. You step back from her, hold her off with power as she stares at you with fear in her eyes, the flames singing the grass of her back yard, the flames devouring you from the inside out as you rise into the sky and scream your life away into the fire—

My mother falls back from me with a cry, hands over her face, skin and clothing smoking, a small fire starting in her hair. She ignores it as Baird rushes to her, sorcery crushing the flames as he curses softly under his breath. But my mother continues to stare at me, now crying, weeping as she covers her mouth with her shaking hands.

"You've changed it," she whispers.

I shake my head, heart pounding. "No," I say, understanding the dual vision. "I've divided it." I reach for more flame, though I sense the edge of temptation is close and that I might not come back from it this time. But I must know all of the story. Instead of keeping it to myself, I reach for all of them, the witches, my mother and her group, Piers. I have no idea if this will work, but we all need to see the stakes—

—You watch, detached and distant, as Liander goes to war with the dragons. But this time there is no shining woman riding the back of their leader, no flare of rainbow light. The mighty creatures

fall, one by one, crushed under his magic until they are no more while the maji—for it must be they, Iepa weeping among them— watch and do nothing—

She is the savior, you send to the others and they echo agreement as the vision unfolds. *Without her, all is lost.*

—Los Angeles is on fire, flames raging through the normal world while flaring piles of witches burn, stakes jutting into the uncaring sky, the ground barren and laid waste in darkness.

To another place, where a red-skinned race with curving black horns lie dead, the Brotherhood in their black robes drawing the life from a tear-shaped energy source, as it sings its final song of agony.

To a green space where a massive storm wreaks havoc, wind tearing at the falling fairy race who collapse and decay before your eyes, the Brotherhood there, always there, to devour the energy of their death.

Cities, towns on fire, a pale-skinned Queen fading to a mummy and then to dust, a giant werewolf crushed and bled dry at the foot of his throne. The world is on fire, the expended power swept into a spinning, central vortex, everything light and good sucked dry until only emptiness remains.

To a tiny chamber, made of stone, and a gold-gilt sarcophagus covered in rainbow light. You drift closer, look inside, and see her face, her eyes closed, hands folded over her breast, Syd's power lost at last to the Brotherhood.

And finally a boy with red-blonde hair and eyes that flash green, standing next to a gap in the Universe as darkness approaches—

TWENTY-THREE

The fire flares, hitting me like a slap across the face as I pull free of the vision to the sound of weeping. My mother's face is in her hands, her shoulders shaking. She looks so tiny, so vulnerable, I can't resist going to her, putting my arms around her, whispering to her soothing sounds until she stills.

"All this time," she chokes against my shoulder as she embraces me at last, "I believed you would be the end of all of us, Zoe. But I couldn't bear to harm you." She shivers as she pulls away and looks up into my eyes. "Every vision I had led to the same place—no matter how much I wanted to change it—to you destroying the Universe." She steps away from me, both hands wiping angrily at tears on her face. "Now I see he was manipulating me, too. Though how, I don't know."

"I do." My mind goes to Gaia and her final gift. "Through the power he stole. Through Gaia's magic. He and his kind have been influencing our visions for centuries, since Sibyl sold us out to them." Leyea stares, shock on her face. "But it doesn't matter, not anymore. We have to help these people, Mother."

She nods quickly, gestures to Baird who is, for the first time, rather contrite when he finally meets my eyes. "We have to find Liander," she says. "And I know where to start."

Tallah steps forward, scowling, hands clasped tightly together. "We're coming with you."

I don't allow protest. "This is our fight," I say. "All of us." And no one argues with me.

Piers grabs my hand as I call up the flame. Mother stares at me and I realize I no longer need my lighter, haven't required it for some time now. She shakes her head, but tries a little smile and I smile in return.

"To the sanctuary," I say, and dive into the fire.

It releases me easily, eagerly even and I wonder if it wants Liander found as much as I do. Makes sense, ultimately, considering his plan will mean the end of all other magicks. I can only hope we are in time to make sure his plans don't succeed.

I have faith my power wouldn't show me a fate that wasn't changeable.

My feet echo hollowly on the stone floor as I step

out, Piers at my side, into the main hall outside the chapel. It takes me a moment to realize the silence in the space isn't just from the early evening hour. As I turn a slow circle, reaching for the hearts and souls of the Oracles who live here, I realize the truth.

They are gone. All of them. Not a single heartbeat remains in the sanctuary, my family disappeared. Grief at their loss hits me hard, though I chose to abandon them, didn't I, not so long ago? I wish my mind wouldn't take me to worst case scenario, though I can only think Liander has them and is using them for some foul part of his plot.

I catch a faint glimmer of life and turn for the chapel door, racing inside. My feet skid on the rock as I slip and almost fall at the edge of one of the benches, the sight of blonde hair tumbling over the side pulling me to a halt.

Ash is unconscious, her heart beat steady, if weak, eyes closed. She appears unhurt physically, but I can't reach her with my mind. My gaze lifts to Rupe who crouches next to her, staring at me with flat dislike.

"Saved her," he says. "Your turn."

I promised him, though it was a different bargain, another life I wanted rescued. Still, I owe him for this, enough to try.

Baird pushes me out of the way, lifts Ash into his arms. She looks so tiny stretched out over his thick forearms, head resting on his shoulder. The way he looks down at her with tenderness and hurt, I have my answer what she means to him.

Rupe shuffles forward, sniffs the air between us. "All gone," he says.

"Do you know where?" My mother interrupts, glances back and forth between Rupe and me.

He shakes his head, scratches at one ear like a dog with a flea bite. When he answers, his tone is mournful, lost. "Why would they leave me?"

How very sad and lonely he is at that moment, a boy abandoned, and I can't help but feel compassion for him. My hand rises, fingers brushing over his face as I let out the flames.

He screams, falls back from me as the fire finds the wolf in him and isolates it. How odd it feels, like an infection, a diseased tumor he carries. But even as the flames try to burn it up, it wriggles free and scatters, and the deeper I dig, the more damage I do until I finally have to retreat.

Rupe pants, still sobbing half breaths, hanging from the seat of the bench with one arm, his entire body smoking. I sag before him, shaking my head, wishing there was something I could do.

But when I look up to apologize, to find a way to comfort him, he is staring at me with utter adoration. He falls to his knees, bending to press his head in my lap, hands stroking my thighs with loving gestures.

"The pain," he whispers. "It's gone."

I pat his head, weariness overwhelming me a moment. Strong hands settle on my shoulders, and I look up into Piers's troubled gray eyes.

"There's no one here," he says. "We have to keep looking."

He's right, of course. I pull away from Rupe who follows me with a hopeful smile. I might have freed him from his pain, but his mind is still broken and I doubt he will ever be whole again.

"Where now?" Tallah is clearly anxious, blue flames snapping over her hands as though she's constantly testing her power. She seems to have no trouble using it here, at least, so whatever is going on has to be focused on her house.

Which gives me an idea. "Your place," I say. "And we need to hurry."

The moment we step out into Tallah's kitchen, I know we've made the right choice, and that we're not alone. Though whether putting ourselves directly in the line of fire is a good thing or not remains to be seen.

I'm not surprised to find Liander sitting at her kitchen counter, helping himself to a cup of coffee while Kayden and a few of the other young sorcerers lounge on her sofa. Anna stands off to one side, mute but furious, wrapped up in visible vines of black power while the rest of Tallah's witches lie unconscious on the floor.

"How delightful." Liander is all posh and arrogance, clearly believing himself to be in the position of power here. I pull in my flame and wait my turn, knowing it will come. I just have to be ready. "Zoe, you made it." He has a lighter in his hand. A shining gold lighter. My heart tightens as I realize I left Sibyl's focus of power here, in this house, for him to find. "And Sibyl thought you wouldn't show. Isn't that right, my dear?"

I turn slowly, stare down the woman I thought my grandmother as she and a few of my Oracle family emerge from one of the bedrooms. The control I had over her slips and falls away, the awakening of her flame bursting to life as Liander tosses the gold lighter across the room to Sibyl's waiting hands. Rena hovers, glaring at me like a furious puppy, and I give her about that much attention.

Sibyl looks terrible despite the return of her power, her face tight and mask-like, shoulders hunched and I wonder if she's finally understanding what selling her soul and those of my people to a man like Liander actually means.

"Have you seen the truth yet?" I've never felt so calm, the fire hugging me close. "Do you know his true aim, Sibyl?" I throw the images from the vision I shared with my mother at her, hitting her with them like the blades of knives. She flinches over and over, eyes widening so far

I'm sure they'll pop from her head at any moment. "Do you understand where you've led the Helios Oracles?"

She shakes her head, but doesn't back down. If anything, her shoulders square, her face composing while the others of our family look to her with nervous eyes, even Rena. "I will follow the path of my visions," she says with conviction I doubt she really feels. If anything, she's resigned herself to the fate before her. "As will our family."

"So you say," my mother steps forward to the gasps of some of the Oracles with Sibyl. "But unless they can see the truth, how can they truly choose?" My mother repeats my performance, only aiming the foresight and her flames at the Helios women gathered at Sibyl's side.

This time, the results are much more satisfying. With the exception of two, they leave Sibyl, fleeing out the open patio door, shrieking as the truth finally overtakes them. The cowards. Though part of me understands their impulse to run from the truth they had betrayed everything our family stood for, duplicitous or not. Only Rena and one other, a tiny, young cousin named Treshi, remain, though the little girl seems more confused than committed.

Sibyl's fire rises, but I am ready to counter her. "Do you really want to fail again so soon?" I let her feel what's inside me and she crumbles at last when the remains of Gaia's power pushes against her.

Even as the former leader of the Helios family falls to her knees and wails in despair, Liander begins a long, slow clap. I turn to him as he finishes his applause, his sorcerers grinning as my cousins weep next to Sibyl.

"What a lovely display of theatrics." Liander sips his coffee before shoving the cup aside so hard it shatters against the wall. He rises and adjusts his tie, a smirk pulling his goatee askew. "I've really enjoyed the performance, but I'm afraid it's time to get down to business."

"What have you done?" Tallah's voice vibrates with anger, her magic spluttering once again. I reach outward with my flames, feel the pressure of his dark power smothering this house.

"Not I," he says. "At least, not alone." His grin splits his face, evil glittering in his eyes. "As a matter of fact, your Council Leader and I have come to an arrangement I'm certain will benefit all of us." His smile fades as he looks at me. "That is, if you don't resist."

Tallah's teeth grind together audibly. "I don't believe you."

He shrugs, suddenly casual and carefree. "You don't have to," he says. "But I assure you, Coven Leader Hensley, you will submit. Or be destroyed."

I'm braced for an attack, but against Tallah. So I'm startled when his power slams full into me, pulling on my fire.

I should be afraid as his sorcery burrows into me, the magic of his minions attacking the others at the same time. But I'm not, not in the least. I sense the struggles around me, know we'll fall, that Liander has found another power source to keep him going. One that feels like witch magic, full of the touch of the elements. But I'm not thinking about him or failure or death.

Not when the power of Gaia tingles through me and feeds my flames.

He can't contain me. I know it the moment the sparks of maji power rise, her soul magic filling me with the greatest joy I've ever known. Liander's face blanches as he falls back, shocked and I laugh in his face as the fire takes me.

Come. I know that voice. I turn inside the flame, see Iepa waiting for me, hand outstretched. I take it, journey with her deeper into the fire, further into the sparks of what was once Gaia.

And then.

And then I see everything.

From the tiniest grain of sand created a million years ago on a far distant plane to the final, brief blink of light as the Universe dies, it's all there, surrounding me in layers and circles and zig-zags of promise and possibility. My mind should rupture from all this knowledge but I watch and contemplate with only mild curiosity while Ipea looks on.

But Iepa isn't alone. I know those two dear faces, Bellanca smiling at me, Thanos nodding slowly as I recognize them and acknowledge their presence.

You're not Oracles. I don't speak, but they hear me.

We actually are, Bellanca's smile makes me grin through my calm. *The first Oracles. You, my dear Zoe, are our creation.*

Should I be freaked out? I find her answer delightful. *Thank you.*

Thanos laughs, but the sound is lost. I only hear it in my head. *You're welcome.*

Who are you, then? Where is my fear and concern for the future? Lost in the endless, timeless flow of space around me.

We have many names, Bellanca says, *but the most recent is Fate.*

I rather like Thanos, he says with a wink.

We were here when the Creator began, Bellanca says, *and we will be the last to go when the Universe dies.*

And maybe not even then, Thanos says.

Maybe. His sister smiles up at him. *For now, all you need to know is we are here to guide you, Zoe. You are our daughter, our sister, our instrument. Through you fate will take either one path or another.*

All you have to do, Thanos says, *is choose.*

Choose what? I shake my head. *You manipulated me.* I'm not angry, but it's true. What a life I've led, full of deceit and lies.

We allowed you to believe we were family, Bellanca says. *And, as far as we're concerned, it's the truth.*

I smile and accept, because there is nothing else I can do.

But we're not here to talk about our little deception, Zoe. There's a problem, and I think you know what it is. Bellanca's steady gaze isn't white here. She has blue eyes, eyes that seem to see right through me, ignoring the swirling layers of future and past and present all waiting for acknowledgement. I nod, calm returning.

The Brotherhood.

But she shakes her head. *No, Zoe,* Bellanca says. *The Oracles.*

That doesn't sound right. *We're not the enemy.* Or are we?

My sister is being obtuse, as always. Thanos shrugs. His eyes are green. How odd. Shouldn't they also be blue? *Your people's purpose was skewed, Zoe, a long time ago.*

By the Brotherhood. So I was right.

By Sibyl and her hate for Gaia. Bellanca's sadness shivers through my composure. *It was she who altered the fate of the Oracles and led us to this place. Had she not given in to her need for power and control, most of what has come to pass would have been unnecessary.* I see flashes of images, of Syd and another woman with ice blue eyes and black hair, facing off in a small stone chamber. *With the guidance of the Oracles, witches would have never succumbed to the terrible punishments of the*

Brotherhood in the Dark Ages. In fact, destiny would have led normals to know of and accept the presence of paranormals among them.

How tragic. I feel the sadness of it, but nothing can rattle my steady quiet for long. *What would you have me do? In this moment,* Bellanca says, *you are the crossroads. In your hands lies the fate of all Oracles.*

Why me? How oddly petulant.

Thanos grins at me. *Why not you?*

I accept that answer without a moment's hesitation. It must be someone. Why not me indeed?

My choices? I don't need them to see—I have all of creation spread out around me. Instead, I focus on the future and what can be—

—the last of the Oracles die quietly, powerless, their fires burned out while the world marches silently on, grim and dark—

—or—

—you rise in sheets of fire consumed by the flames while your people's magic is cleansed and reborn, greatness unfolding for the magic races of all planes in their wake—

So. I turn to them again, a tiny pulse of regret in my heart. *I let my people die out, take their power and it will be as though the Helios Oracles never existed.*

Doing so will ensure no one ever uses them for ill gain again, Bellanca says. *If they are allowed to continue this path, Liander Belaisle and his dark master will win.*

Liander has a master beyond himself? I didn't know,

though when I turn to examine that possibility, Thanos's voice draws me back.

Or, he says.

I nod. *I die,* I say, *using the power of Gaia to cleanse the hold of the Brotherhood over my family and allowing them to see the true future for the first time in centuries.*

And guide this Universe into a new age. Bellanca's soft smile is tinged with sadness. *You understand your choices?*

I do. They are rather simple, after all. My family's end, or mine, for the sake of the Universe.

I'm ready. I step into the fire at my feet as Iepa raises one hand.

My sister's power is the key, she says as I enter the flames. *Remember what I told you, that you must save her regardless of what you decide.* Syd, yes, of course. Iepa's voice is desperate, but she shares a burst of love. *And thank you, Zoe Helios. No matter your choice.*

TWENTY-FOUR

I open my eyes, know as I draw a breath only a fraction of a moment has passed. Liander is falling back from me, swearing as Kayden and his sorcerers scramble to their feet, fear radiating outward from them. I've already made my choice, know there can only be one path, one way for me to make things right. Or as right as possible, to repent for the sins of Sibyl and her jealousy and hate.

Liander must know what's coming, see it in my face, perhaps, as my fire roars forward, plunging toward him. He tries to shield, but he's far too weak, the flames of fate coming for him as they never have before. But I'm so wrapped up in calm I see his future too late, and in doing so, in watching the vision of what he will become unfold while he fights off my fire, I allow him to slip through my fingers.

The black tunnel snaps shut behind him, leaving the handful of young sorcerers to stare after their fleeing master. Kayden is the first to react and I sigh, let him go, though Piers lunges to go after him and his cohorts.

"Let it be," I say, accepting the future that is to come, knowing what I must do next is the only way to hope to counter what I've seen. Liander's dark master will bring horror and destruction to this place.

I can't allow that to happen.

The flames rise, consuming me with glee and abandon as I stride outside into the darkness. I have far to go if I'm to reach her and must begin my journey before it's too late.

Someone hisses behind me, their touch searing a hold on my skin for an instant. I turn to face my aunt, Ash trembling from fatigue, but her face dark with worry.

"Fight it, Zo." She clutches at Baird who holds her up, looking at me with worried eyes. "Don't let go now."

I shake my head at her, smile, let her see I'm all right, that this is my decision. "I have to go, Ash." I raise my hand to Tallah and her witches and she waves back, face sad. Piers stares, stunned, but with growing fear on his face. He steps down from the deck and into the sand, looking at my mother, at Ash, at me.

"What's going on?" His voice shakes ever so slightly.

"The fire is taking her." My mother's tone is remarkably steady, her smile firm but gentle. "You've seen the future." Not a question.

I nod. "Our people must be free." I feel them, newly fled, coming to listen, returning with nowhere else to go, to watch me as the fire rises further, dancing around me in hypnotic waves of flame. "And there is only one way for the Oracles of Helios to rise again."

Piers suddenly understands, or at least thinks he does from the horrified look on his face. "Zoe, no. Do what Ash said. Fight it."

They just don't get it. But my mother does. "You've been here, where I am."

She nods, looks away. "I was weak. I failed. And would have died."

"No," I say. "You didn't have everything you needed. That was why you couldn't satisfy fate. It would have been a waste of your life, Mother."

Is that relief on her face? Gratitude? "I have always loved you," she says. "And done what I could to protect you."

"Even when you thought I was a monster." I smile, nod. "I know that now." I turn from her and can't bring myself to meet Piers's eyes, though the calm remains. There's too much sorrow in him. He can't love me like I love him. He's only really just gotten to know me ever so little. And yet, fate works in funny ways.

I only wish I'd had a chance to get to know him—myself, without the visions—before the end.

Piers takes a step closer, heart breaking almost audibly. I can't let him go further.

I reach for Gaia as Piers leaps at me. But he's too late, the flames carry me up, into the sky, and I'm soaring.

My vision widens, and I can see it all, the network web of darkness woven around the blue of witch power, forming domed caves of black over the continent. I try to ride the fire to the familiar yard from my vision, but I can't break through the mesh of sorcery holding pattern over each territory. And the fire wants me to fly. So I fly.

Forward, toward the first light of dawn, her power pulling me onward. She's easy to find, a pinpoint of rainbow light, a tiny territory in Pennsylvania untouched by the black, though it crowds around her, a hulking giant of darkness lurking, ready to pounce and put out her brilliance with its crushing weight.

Her light calls me even as the flames roar brighter and I feel, at last, the first pain of their consumption. I'm almost out of time, my calm cracking in thin spider webs of agony as I cry out, the voice of a raptor, before plunging down to the earth.

I slam into the grass, my body raging with agony now, staggering me. Fear wakes, the last of my reserve broken and scattered. Whatever held me in that place of calm has abandoned me in the end and I can only weep tears of flame as I collapse to the grass and burn.

Despite the pain, I hear the slam of a screen door, the footfalls of her approach. I don't have to open my eyes to know it's her. It's Syd, watching me with mouth agape, her power wrapped around her like a cloak, ready to defend her family.

The fire retreats, just enough I can sit up, look at her through crackling flames. She doesn't try to touch me with power and I'm glad. If she offered me a way out now, I'm afraid I'd break and take it. I must be strong. But she has to be warned.

The pressure of sorcery against her boundaries is almost too much for me to bear, the fire rising to defy it. How can she not feel them coming for her? She has but moments, heartbeats. I'm too late to save her.

"RUN!" I shove an image of darkness at her, hit her with my fear and the black. She flinches, almost speaks, but I can't let her doubt. "Sydlynn Hayle, if you love your family, run and don't look back!"

I have no more time. The flames are angry with me now, for making them wait, driving me upward into the sky again. I look down, just in time to see a bright flare of rainbow magic, a mere moment before the black pounces and drags her under.

And then I can't weep for her or anyone else, not with the fire taking me. I'm crumbling from the inside, hollowing out, though the pain increases with each moment until I feel I cannot take any more, will not survive another moment as I plunge back toward the west, to the call of the seabirds and the sand and the pounding ocean. Wings of flame spread out from my shoulders, filling the night with orange light, reaching out to each and every Oracle as my power connects with theirs and burns them clean.

I sigh through my agony at their freedom, their glowing light. They will be so much more. And I have given them back their future.

My last task complete, I give in to the fire and plummet, out of control and near the end, to crash into the white sand.

He's there, I can hear him calling my name, weeping for me, even as the fire happily licks its way through the last thoughts in my mind and swallows me whole.

EPILOGUE

He's still weeping. The sound wakes me from the dark as an ember fires to the sound. The edge of the coal cracks, breaks apart, sizzling on the wet beach. I stretch outward, calling the flames. They answer me, coy, sated, but eager enough to awaken. My body comes together from silicone and carbon, siphoned from the sand, the water, the air around me. I can choose whatever shape I will, but I miss my old one. It's the face he knows.

His weeping cuts off as I rise and shake off the last of the ash, a flare of flame washing me clean. Piers stares, barely breathing as I cross to him, take his hands in mine, pull him to his feet. And kiss him with the heat of the fire that's made me new again. "Zoe," he whispers into my mouth.

"Phoenix," I say.

Like what you read? Find out more at
pattilarsen.com

Syd's back in an all new adventure!

Here's a look at the first chapter of
Book One of the
Hayle Coven Destinies

THE OUTCAST

ONE

I dodged to the left, dipping my head over Max's rough shoulder as the wide-open mouth of our attacker spewed neon green acid in my direction. My shields shuddered under the touch of the potent fluid, bursting into flame and smoke, washed away in the beating of my drach friend's giant wing strokes.

The ball of rainbow magic in my hand sizzled in my palm as I took aim on the nasty critter now winding its way beneath us and tried to focus. *A little lower, Max.* He obliged immediately, banking to the left and dipping his massive, gray scaled head. Right in the path of my throw. *You're blocking my view.*

My apologies. He actually sounded like he was having fun. Imagine. Then again, as he turned his big noggin to the right, long neck snaking his face out of the way, I had to admit the thrilling bubble in my stomach was my very own brand of excitement.

Seriously, Hayle. Get a grip already.

The reptile-like creature slithered through the air, clearing Max's bulk. Shining teeth made up most of its scaled face, two pin-points of black eyes and one bare slit just above the glittering fangs were almost lost in the gaping of its mouth. A high-pitched squeal assaulted my ears, making it down to my bones, sending shivers through me. Wingless, flying by power alone, it twisted sideways, thin, ribbon like body snapping into a multi-hued coil. Spit sizzled another round of its horrible venom our way.

My shields could handle it. This particular creature might be slippery, but they weren't all that clever. As though he was reading my mind—and perhaps he was, at that—Max turned over on his side, one wing over my head, giving me a nice, clear view of the pale lavender horizon and two suns cresting the distant mountains. And, even better, the monstrosity attacking us.

Perfect.

My arm drew back even as my power built inside the hissing ball of magic. While it wasn't necessary for me to actually throw the weapon, I took great satisfaction from doing so.

With the practiced pitch of long experience, I let the ball of multi-colored fire fly, letting out a whoop of success as it impacted solidly in the center of the twisting creature's face. Its squeal was muffled this time, not the penetrating nasty I'd been enduring since this fight began. The rainbow power of my attack split into ribbons, forming a net of magic around the creature's head, smothering it. Tail thrashing, it fell beneath us, plunging to the deep purple lake below, a large splash marking its passing.

My hand swiped at a trickle of sweat running down the side of my face as I patted Max's scaled shoulder. *Nicely done, big man.*

Not so bad yourself, my friend. He turned in a slow arc, both of us watching his people far below. Only a handful or so of the odd creatures remained to be dealt with, a far cry from the hundreds of twisting, vicious whatever they were that showed up as a pack last night. At least, I think it was last night. It was so easy to lose track of time when I was on other planes, fighting with the drach.

Brilliant idea luring them here, I sent as Max hovered in place. His big head turned toward me, one diamond eye spinning with power.

Indeed, he sent. *I had hoped our current strategy of drawing them to an empty plane might make our job easier.*

Did it ever. Hard enough fighting these creatures who crossed over from the other Universe, but doing so in the veil made tracking them all down almost impossible. At least if we managed to lure them to a plane and force them to cross in our wake or drive them through an opening we created, we could trap them and deal with them in a contained environment. We had, as yet, to discover a species who could use the veil on their own, so it worked most of the time.

Should we do a sweep to see if we missed any? Wow, did I actually sound eager? Max had the good sense not to tease me about it. But, damn it, this was fun.

Yeah, I admitted it. Fun. Sigh. Something was seriously wrong with me.

I believe we captured the entire swarm, he sent, faint amusement in his mental voice. *Your assistance is appreciated, as usual, Sydlynn Hayle.*

Weariness had begun to set in and as I rolled my throwing shoulder, eyes scanning the drach cleaning up the last of the mess below, I realized I was tired. Tired and sore and probably ready to go home after all.

Any time, I sent as Max raised his head and widened his wings, thrusting upward. A gap appeared in the veil, shimmering around the edges with the glitter of diamonds as he plunged us through. It felt weird to be in the veil again, the muffled darkness hugging me close as the slice sealed shut behind us. Until the next time.

Max grunted in my head. *Is it just me*, he sent, *or does it seem no matter how hard we try, we are unable to eradicate the threats let through when the veil between Universes was damaged?*

I didn't want to go there, had actually dreaded the

conversation. Because I knew where it was going. The giant first race of drach were the most powerful creatures in the Universe—in our Universe, anyway—and though their leader was a very dear friend, I still felt uneasy reminding myself all of this mess was kind of my fault.

Okay, so Fate had a lot to do with it. From my purposeful creation and development from ordinary witch to powerful maji, the discovery of my drach heritage and the fact everything I went through to get to this point was, as it turned out, fated long before I was born, I suppose I shouldn't have felt any guilt over our present predicament. My son, Gabriel, may have opened the way between the two Universes, but it was Max and his people who divided them in the first place, wasn't it?

Syd. Max's voice was soft in my head. *I'm sorry. I know where your mind is going.*

I shifted on his back, uncomfortable that he knew, though I patted his neck ridge so he would know I wasn't angry. *It's okay*, I sent. And sighed. *We all played a part, didn't we?*

We did, he sent, body effortless in the vastness of the veil, soaring over glittering divisions between planes. Every time I came into the rubbery membrane separating the worlds of my Universe, I was in awe of just how vast this place really was. But it couldn't distract me today, not with my mind going where I'd tried to keep it from wandering. My son's kidnapping and subsequent control by Ameline Benoit could not have been avoided. I still cringed at the memory of the loss of my first husband, Liam. Gabriel's father's death was also fated, damn them. *But you won, in the end, as you always do,* Max's mental voice broke my whirling thought process. *And I know we will succeed now.*

It's been seven years, Max. I leaned forward and rested my forehead on his neck, weariness washing over me in waves. *You would think we'd have made some headway by now.*

Perhaps if Demonicon's Node hadn't fallen, he sent, banking right as we neared my home plane at last. *But the damage done when Meira was forced to rebuild it let even more creatures through.*

I remembered. My sister's fight to become true Ruler of Demonicon almost broke her and the entire Universe. But she made it through, was stronger for it.

How long do you think we'll have to keep doing this? Oh, Syd. Syd. So transparent my eagerness, even when weary from this most recent fight.

A while yet, Max sent. *I'm certain there are still many more creatures who escaped the Dark Universe and came here, now hiding among the planes.*

We'd encountered a few that weren't a threat and left them alone on abandoned planes. But the harmless ones were few and far between. I had no desire to visit the Dark Universe—even if that was possible—if all they bred were violent, nasty and dangerous creatures like the ones we'd fought over the years.

I wonder how many of our own creatures crossed into their Universe? It had been on my mind for a while.

There is no way of knowing, he sent as the air before him split and gaped wide, his body shifting, shrinking even as we plunged forward toward the darkened basement on the other side of the rift. *Though from the empty planes we've been uncovering, I fear we've lost whole civilizations to the other side.*

I hope they are okay. I leaped from his back as he stepped out into the quiet, my sneakers squeaking on the concrete. Max's diamond eyes glowed as he smiled a little at me, gray toned face softly marked with tiny scales. He bowed his bald head.

"As do I." His deep voice matched the rumble of his mental one, the edges of it touched by the hint of the song of the drach. I hugged him, impulsive, my shoulders aching from the battle, but I didn't care. Max embraced me with his powerful arms, the powder scent of him touched with a hint of smoke from the fight. His gray robe was soft under my cheek as he spoke again. "We do what we can, Syd."

I nodded into his chest before leaning back and stepping away. Bitterness bubbled and I did my best to contain it, rubbing at the goosebumps that rose on my arms. "Would be nice to have a little help," I grumbled.

Max sighed, a soft sound that nonetheless stirred the air around me. I wondered sometimes if his human shape actually hid the dragon within, like an illusion. Everything about Max was larger than life. "The maji," he said.

Damned, cursed, wretched maji. "You'd think for once they'd get off their sorry asses and give us a hand." I did my best most times to forget about the pathetic race I'd become part of. But, I shared none of their refusal to act. The second race of the Universe, they feared interference and, no matter what the risk facing us, had always refused to assist.

Cowards, the lot of them.

Max's smile was gone, but his gentle presence helped me settle down.

"A time will come," he said, "when even they will be forced to admit their need to act." I highly doubted that, but I was too tired to argue. "For now, we are more than enough." I grinned at him, nodded. Way to make me feel better. "I will let you rest," he said. "Be well, my friend."

"You, too." I waved as he turned and entered the gap, hugging myself as it sealed behind him, leaving me alone in the quiet of the basement under my house.

Well, mostly alone.

I turned to face the one waiting for me, not sure if I should expect a lecture or not.

ABOUT THE AUTHOR

Everything you need to know about me is in this one statement: I've wanted to be a writer since I was a little girl, and now I'm doing it. How cool is that, being able to follow your dream and make it reality? I've tried everything from university to college, graduating the second with a journalism diploma (I sucked at telling real stories), am part of an all-girl improv troupe (if you've never tried it, I highly recommend making things up as you go along as often as possible). I've even been in a Celtic girl band (some of our stuff is on YouTube!) and was an independent film maker. My life has been one creative thing after another—all leading me here, to writing books for a living.

Now with multiple series in happy publication, I live on beautiful and magical Prince Edward Island (I know you've heard of Anne of Green Gables) with my very patient husband and multitude of pets.

I love-love-love hearing from you! You can reach me (and I promise I'll message back) at patti@pattilarsen.com. And if you're eager for your next dose of Patti Larsen books (usually about one release a month) come join my mailing list! All the best up and coming, giveaways, contests and, of course, my observations on the world (aren't you just dying to know what I think about everything?) all in one place: http://smarturl.it/PattiLarsenEmail.

Last—but not least!—I hope you enjoyed what you read! Your happiness is my happiness. And I'd love to hear just what you thought. A review where you found this book would mean the world to me—reviews feed writers more than you will ever know. So, loved it (or not so much), **your honest review would make my day**. Thank you!